PRAISE FOR *JUST A DROP OF WATER*

"9/11 reverberates in a middle-school boy's life, thrusting him into a bigger and more threatening world. This is history tensely told for readers too young to remember the moment when this century truly began."

—Richard Peck, author of *On the Wings of Heroes*

"Tackling a difficult topic, Kerry O'Malley Cerra captures the mood of the country right after September 11 in a way that's not frightening or sensationalized. This well-told, poignant novel about prejudice, school bullying, and best friends should spark discussion and capture the hearts of young readers for a very long time."

—Augusta Scattergood, author of *Glory Be*

"Memorable characters bring to life a story of friends who, after the tragedy of September 11, must confront the darker side of their community, their families, and their hearts. Kerry Cerra is definitely a debut author to watch!"

—Christina Diaz Gonzalez, author of *The Red Umbrella, A Thunderous Whisper,* and *Moving Target*

"Kerry O'Malley Cerra has written a novel that is both brave and true. In showing us the darker sides of ourselves when confronted with tragedy and fear, her characters lead us to the light."

—Laurie Calkhoven, author of *Michael at the Invasion of France, 1943* and the Boys of Wartime series

"This touching story is like the legend of the origami paper cranes, a symbol of peace, which states that if you fold one thousand of them, your heart's desire will come true."

—Kathryn Fitzmaurice, author of
A Diamond in the Desert

"*Just a Drop of Water* brings this generation's young readers a glimpse of September 11 that is both thought-provoking and real."

—Caroline Starr Rose, author of *May B.* and *Blue Birds*

"The supplemental material middle-grade history teachers are looking for. . . . A perceptive exploration of an event its audience already sees as history."

—*Kirkus Reviews*

"Historical fact and realistic fiction elements are woven together with an expert hand, making readers care about this moment in history and giving educators an excellent book sure to spur thoughtful discussion."

—*School Library Journal*

"Two boys have maturity thrust upon them in this deeply engaging and thoughtful book."

—*VOYA*

JUST A DROP of WATER

Kerry O'Malley Cerra

Sky Pony Press
New York

Sky Pony Press books may be purchased in bulk at special discounts for sales promotion, corporate gifts, fund-raising, or educational purposes. Special editions can also be created to specifications. For details, contact the Special Sales Department, Sky Pony Press, 307 West 36th Street, 11th Floor, New York, NY 10018 or info@skyhorsepublishing.com.

Sky Pony® is a registered trademark of Skyhorse Publishing, Inc.®, a Delaware corporation.

Visit our website at www.skyponypress.com.

10 9 8 7 6 5 4 3 2

Library of Congress Cataloging-in-Publication Data

Cerra, Kerry O'Malley.
Just a drop of water / Kerry O'Malley Cerra.
    pages cm
Summary: "Jake and Sam are best friends, but after the attacks on September 11, their friendship is in danger of crumbling as Sam and his family succumb to hatred for being Muslim American"-- Provided by publisher.
ISBN 978-1-62914-613-3 (hardback)
[1. Best friends--Fiction. 2. Friendship--Fiction. 3. September 11 Terrorist Attacks, 2001--Fiction. 4. Arab Americans--Fiction. 5. Muslims--Fiction. 6. Conduct of life--Fiction. 7. Family life--Florida-- Fiction. 8. Florida--Fiction.] I. Title.
PZ7.O31927Jus 2014
[Fic]--dc23
2014015987

Paperback ISBN: 978-1-5107-1234-8
Ebook ISBN: 978-1-63220-211-6

Cover design by Brian Peterson
Cover art credit Katy Betz

Printed in the United States of America

For Kylie, Josh, & Griffin
You radiate goodness in this world.
I am the luckiest!

JUST A DROP OF WATER

CHAPTER 1

SEPTEMBER 7, 2001
FRIDAY

....

I'd rather dunk my head in a school toilet than run cross country. All the tree branches and roots are like land-mines. They slow me down. Besides, I'm not good for long distances—I'm more of a sprinter. You know, get from point A to point B as fast as possible, with a fin-ish line always in sight and no surprises along the way. That's running. Unfortunately, Coach makes us do cross country in the fall or we can't run track in the spring. It's stupid. They're not the same sport at all.

"Come on, only half a mile left," Sam says as he grabs my elbow and pulls me through the woods. He's not even winded as he adds, "Let's pick up the pace."

Only half a mile? Might as well be three. Sam made me practice all summer, and even though I've gotten a lot better, I still hate cross country. But at least Coach knows how hard we've been working. He's sure to name us team captains; it's only fair and the only reason I'm letting Sam drag me along. To top it all off, we're going to crush Palmetto Ridge Middle—and Tyler Montgomery—this year. That's why I keep running.

The trees block out the sun, but the air is still sticky. It feels like a hundred degrees and my shirt's soaked. Dodging a tree limb, I pant, "I. HATE. YOU."

"I know, Jake. You tell me every day. Maybe I'll let you win since it's your birthday. Or not." He laughs and sprints ahead of me.

My eyes dart up and down and side to side, trying to navigate the forest maze. As the woods thin out, the redness of the school track peeks through the edge of the tree line. A smooth run. A painted finish line. I speed up.

The rest of the team is way behind, as usual, including Kirk Steiner. He's the only other eighth grader on the team and he's new . . . and fast, though not as fast as Sam and me. Okay, maybe a little faster, but still, Sam and I have been on the team since sixth grade and we're going to lead it this year.

Kirk hangs back with the seventh graders for our runs. If he tried, I'm sure he'd be able to keep pace with

Sam and me up front, but he likes to show off. He stays back and then blows us away at the last minute.

Leaves crunch under my feet as I just about exit the woods. Before I pass the last tree, Sam pops out and ambushes me.

"So predictable," I shout. We wrestle each other to the ground. Sam's solid like a cannon and I'm more like a bayonet. Doesn't matter though—we're almost always opposites. I'm faster, but Sam can run longer. I have blonde hair, blue eyes, and pale skin; Sam's got dark hair, brown eyes, and brown skin. He can throw a bomb of a pass in football and I'm the best receiver. We make a great team. Together, we're unstoppable.

Sam pins me. I squirm to the left, break free, and flip him to the side.

He shakes dirt from his hair. "Nice move!"

Sweat drips into my eye and I wipe it with my sleeve. "I've been saving that one just for you."

The team passes us and Sam looks at his watch. "Come on. You're gonna be late for your own party."

Dinner at home, with Grandma and Sam's family, is hardly a party, but it's all I want this year. Well, that, and tickets to a Philadelphia Eagles game. In Philly!

We scramble to our feet. With the team ahead of us, Sam and I take off.

"We got this!" I yell, as we streak by them.

Sam taps Kirk on the back as he passes him. "Race ya!"

That's all Kirk needs to hear. He pulls away from the group and speeds toward us, faster than a blitzkrieg attack.

The air's so humid I feel like I'm in a foggy bathroom. I breathe in deep. Sam's usually ahead of me by now, but our wrestling match gave us an even start at the edge of the woods. There are no more holes. No roots. No branches. This is the part I'm good at. I pump my arms harder and extend my legs completely. I am flying. But so is Kirk. Steps from the finish line, he and I are tied so I stretch my neck out, hoping the inches are enough to beat him, but they're not. Kirk's legs are longer. He's like a machine—like someone clicks an autopilot button and he just goes.

Kirk wins.

I finally beat Sam for the first time since we've been running cross country, only to end up in second place anyway. Crazy. I have to give Kirk props, though; he totally killed that. Sam and I are going to have to train harder—we can't let the new kid show us up.

I lace my hands on top of my head and pace. Sam's hunched over trying to catch his breath, but Kirk's barely winded.

One of the seventh graders says, "That was awesome. It looked like you guys were running from a gator or something."

Sam and I crack up. When we were six, he and I saw a baby gator on the bank of the canal down the street from our houses. I wasn't supposed to go there. I wasn't even supposed to leave my fenced-in backyard, but Sam and I snuck out because we were sure there were submarine spies in that water. The little gator was just lying in the sun. Then, all of a sudden, a momma gator shot out of the water and hissed at us. We took off. I'd never been so scared in my life. I'm pretty sure if we'd been chased by a gator today, Sam and I would have beaten Kirk.

Coach Rehart clicks the stop-watch as the last kid comes in. He scribbles some stuff on his clipboard. "Jake, that was one of your better runs. Great job."

Summer training paid off. Sam gives me a high five.

Coach flips a paper over then looks at Sam. "Sameed? Care to explain?"

The only time anyone calls Sam Sameed is on the first day of school when teachers don't yet know he's just Sam. Or when his Dad's mad at him.

Sam shrugs. "I tripped in the woods and lost time."

Good thing he's a quick thinker.

Coach sighs. Then he turns and pats Kirk's shoulder.

"Good time, kid. A little over the numbers that your old coach sent me, but you're probably still adjusting to our humidity."

Kirk nods.

Seriously? He usually runs faster than we've seen this last week? He *is* a machine. I guess that's not a bad thing. I mean, we're sure to go undefeated this year with Kirk, Sam, and me. It'll be great to finally beat Palmetto Ridge, a.k.a. Palmetto Bugs (or just Bugs as Sam calls them). They run dirty. In the thick woods, when no one's watching, they trip kids or push them into the bushes. Tyler Montgomery's the leader of the Bugs. Last year, he pantsed me as he ran by. I tripped on my shorts and must've yelled out before my face hit the ground. Sam, who was in front of me, doubled back to help. I scrambled to my feet and pulled my shorts back up. We tried to catch Tyler, but I was down for too long. We lost the meet, too. A lump rises in my throat remembering it. Tyler's the Bugs' best runner, and next year we'll all be in high school together. But I've decided that I'll never let him beat me again. This year, he and his team are going down!

Yeah, it's good to have Kirk with us. I stick out my fist and he bumps it.

"Huddle around, boys." Coach adjusts his sunglasses. "Next week, on Tuesday . . . uh, that should be the . . . eleventh, we get our shot at Palmetto Ridge."

My stomach flips with both excitement and fear. Sam's got a smile as wide as that momma gator's mouth. Kirk glances around like he's trying to figure out what the big deal is.

I whisper to him, "I'll fill you in later." Maybe I'll invite him to run with Sam and me this weekend.

Coach waves us off. "Remember, practice Monday. We'll be taking our team picture, so wear your jerseys to school." He fumbles with the stopwatch in his hand. "Oh, I almost forgot. Our team captains."

My heart buzzes. Sam and I have been planning this since sixth grade—train hard, keep Coach happy, and lead the team our eighth-grade year.

Coach looks at me, and his face tightens. He's getting ready to call my name, I can feel it. "Kirk, you've been great with helping out the younger teammates since you got here. That's good leadership. Going by that, plus the fastest times, the captains this season will be Sam and Kirk."

Kirk? Seriously?

The seventh graders stare at me. Sam grabs my arm, pulling me away before I can tell Coach how messed up that is.

I wrench myself from Sam's grip. "I practiced all summer for nothing."

Sam shoves me toward the school. "Go get your stuff.

I'll talk to Coach for you. I don't want you saying something dumb and getting kicked off the team."

"I never wanted to be on the team in the first place! I hate cross country."

"Yeah, but you worked too hard to quit now. Besides, you know he'll cut you from track in the spring if you don't run cross country."

Sam's right, but it's still not fair. This is my third year on the team. I did everything I was supposed to do and worked my butt off to get my times down; they're the best they've ever been. If Sam hadn't ambushed me in the woods, we might have both beat Kirk today. But maybe not. The kid is crazy fast. He's headed toward the locker room with the rest of the team, totally dumb to the fact that he just stole my spot. Seriously, what's the point in having a plan when it all just blows up in your face?

....

At home, when I get out of the shower, everyone's already scattered around the dining room table. Dad and Sam's parents—Mr. and Mrs. Madina—are at one end. Sam, his twin sister Aamber, and I sit at the other.

Mom made my favorite foods: mac-n-cheese and hot dogs. She leans over the table, takes away the two extra plates, and motions for us to scoot closer, saying, "Uncle

Hugh and Aunt Margie can't make it. They'll drop your gift off another day."

Uncle Hugh was my grandpa's best friend, but we're not really related. He did a lot for Grandma and Mom after Grandpa died. Now Uncle Hugh's a Florida state representative. Mom's his secretary, which is cool because I get to see him a lot.

Mom sticks her head into the living room and calls to Grandma. "Are you joining us or not?"

Grandma glides in and takes her seat at the adult end of the table. "You are not going to believe what they're saying on TV. CNN is claiming that Mother Teresa had an exorcism before she died."

Mrs. Madina chuckles. "You can't be serious."

Mom reaches for the bowl of macaroni. "I don't believe that. How can a lady who spent her life promoting peace be full of demons? It must be a hoax."

Dad slaps the table. "Well, that's enough news to get my *head spinning*."

Mr. Madina's wearing a Cookie Monster T-shirt and when he busts out laughing at Dad's joke it looks like Cookie Monster's laughing, too.

That's Sam's and my cue to break away from their conversation.

Sam whispers to me. "I talked to Coach about Kirk. He's not budging."

I shrug. "Whatever."

Aamber mumbles through her food, "Kirk, the new kid? He's super cute."

Great. Fast and cute. Aamber's so weird; I seriously have no idea how she and Sam are twins.

Sam pulls the captain armband out of his pocket. "Listen, I came up with a plan on my way home."

Of course he did. We make plans for everything. "What?"

"I'm gonna ask Coach to make all three of us captains or he can give my spot to someone else."

I punch my chest and finally swallow. "You're gonna quit the team?"

"No, I just won't be captain."

Sam's solid. We met in the sandbox at the park the summer before first grade. Both of us happened to be playing with little green army guys and some older kids came over to try to steal them. Sam and I teamed up and threw sand at the kids—which made them run away— and we've been best friends ever since.

I grab his armband and look at it. "Don't do that. You deserve it. I just need to run faster and beat Kirk's times. Maybe Coach will make me captain then."

"I hope so. No matter what, at least you know you'll still lead the track team."

For a second I'm confident, but then say, "What if Kirk tries out for track, too? I'm done."

"Running track's different. It's your thing. Kirk won't take your captain spot there."

I snort.

"What?" Sam takes a sip of his Dr. Pepper.

"Think about it. He's Captain Kirk. Like *Star Trek*."

Sam spews soda out his nostrils and I crack up even more. He holds his nose. "Ow, ow, burning."

"Ugh!" Aamber looks at me. "You know, if your mom hadn't put you in that *special* school, you'd still be in seventh grade. Sam should go with you. You're both so immature."

We laugh even harder.

It was a special school, but not like Aamber thinks. Mom found one that would let me start a year early, though my grades are proof I should have waited another year. Or two.

Mom stands. "Time for cake."

She sets her homemade spice cake with cream cheese frosting in front of me. The best.

Sam's being a goof and sings "Happy Birthday" louder than anyone, hitting notes that could make glass shatter.

Aamber smacks him on the head. "Dork."

This makes him sing even louder and she rolls her eyes.

Mom and Dad stand behind me, and Mrs. Madina snaps a picture of us. When the song's over, Grandma scoots in for a photo, too. I smile as she wraps her arms—bracelet's jangling—around me.

Mom leans in. "Make a wish."

There are so many things I want this year. I want to beat Palmetto. I want to get back at Tyler for embarrassing me last year. I want to win districts. I want to medal again in track. Straight A's would be cool. And a girlfriend would be awesome. I even want those Eagles tickets pretty bad. But what I want right now, more than anything, is to be captain of the cross country team. I earned it.

I blow out the candles—all thirteen in one shot.

....

Mom decked out the rocker with balloons and I sit. Dad hands me an envelope. Plane tickets to Philly for the game? I rip it open and see three tickets to a Miami Dolphins game instead.

Dad sighs. "I hope you like it. We tried for the Eagle's game but we just couldn't swing it."

It was a long shot, and I sort of feel bad even asking

for that to begin with. Dolphin tickets aren't cheap either, and I'm glad they thought of this as a backup plan because, really, any football game is fun. "It's great, thanks!"

Mom says, "They're for you, Dad, and Sam."

Sam jumps up. "For real?" He thanks them and grabs the tickets. "Three Sundays from now against the Raiders." He looks at his parents. "Can I go?"

Mrs. Madina looks at Mom. "If you're sure it's all right."

Mom nods and Sam high fives me before handing me a box. I tear the wrapping off and open the lid. It's the Mario Party Nintendo game. Safe by Mom's wishes, but I know Sam. I open the case as a smile breaks across my face. He's the *best*! The disk reads *Battle Tanx: Global Assault*. Awesome.

Mom gets freaked out about military games—she says war is never a game—so Sam and I only play them at his house. I don't want to make her mad, but seriously, every kid plays them. Maybe she'll loosen up some now that I'm thirteen. "Thanks, Sam. I've been begging for Mario."

He grins.

I move the tissue paper away. There's a *LIFE* magazine featuring Civil War artifacts. My heart races. Sam and I have been looking everywhere for this issue. I yank it out and flip through it.

Mom sighs. My war obsession has always bothered her, even back when I played green army guys with Sam in the sandbox. I'm sure it was because Grandpa died in a battle overseas. She keeps his folded flag in a triangle box on our mantel, but she doesn't like to talk about his death. Every time I ask, she always says, "Talking about that makes me too sad, but I sure wish he got the chance to meet you." Then she'll tell me some story about all the cool things they did together while he was alive.

One time, my parents took me to Disney World for my seventh birthday. All my friends had told me how cool Mr. Toad's Wild Ride was. When we passed by, I begged Mom and Dad to go on it, but right there, in the middle of hundreds of people, Mom teared up. Eventually, we got in line and she told me the story about the first time Grandpa took her to Disney. It was back when you needed tickets for each ride. After Mom rode Mr. Toad's Wild Ride, she begged to go on again, and again, so Grandpa traded people all the D and E tickets—which were the best ones—in his value book for C tickets because that's what you needed to ride Mr. Toad. The next time they went to Disney—the last time before he died—they paid to get in and then only bought C tickets for the whole day, riding Mr. Toad over and over, letting people pass them in line so they could ride in the car named Moley every time, just because it sounded funny and made them laugh.

I put the *LIFE* magazine away; I can look at it later.

I walk over to Mr. Madina. "Thank you."

He shakes my hand. "No problem, Jake. Happy birthday."

I give Mrs. Madina a hug and she says, "Happy birthday, sweetie. I can't believe how fast you're all growing."

I look at Aamber and she shakes her head. She hates our military obsession for way different reasons than Mom. Aamber makes fun of us for our battle plans, mostly because she was always our enemy and suffered through fake interrogations, only to proclaim her innocence and tell us how stupid we were every time. But one time, when we were eight, she asked us to help launch an attack on Mr. Wilkey, the supposed vampire man next door to the Madinas'. She and her friend Katie swore he tried to talk to them through the wooden fence when they were night-swimming. Sam and I immediately set up an Advanced Operations Base in the corner of the porch and dubbed the mission Operation Vampire. It was a joint task force with Sam, the Navy admiral, and me, the Army general. We swam through the swampy pool and climbed the mountainous play set to the top of the monkey bars. Just as we were about to launch missiles (sticks) at Mr. Wilkey's house, Mrs. Madina came out and busted us. It was the first time we'd ever had an unsuccessful mission. After that, we learned to plan for all possible situations that could foil our strategies.

Only I didn't do that with cross country. I'm so stupid. I never thought some new kid, who happened to be faster than me, would join the team. I should have pushed myself harder at practice from the first day Kirk showed up.

Grandma's next and she hands me a small box, then kisses me on the cheek. "This one's extra-special, love. I've been saving it for you for a very long time."

"Really?" I open it. There's a blue ribbon with silver lines down the sides and a silver eagle in the middle; on the bottom hangs a white star circled by five golden eagles. I know this pin. Every time I go to Grandma's, I can't help but stare at Grandpa's medal in its clear case propped on the shelf next to his picture—a real hero. "For me?"

Grandma touches my arm. "You're just like him, you know?"

I love it when she tells me that. I get up and hug her.

Grandma says all sing-songy in my ear, "Just a drop of water." She calls this her mantra, but I can't figure out what it's code for. It's like she uses it in a different way every time.

Mom wipes a tear from her eye and smiles at me. "Take good care of it." She heads for the kitchen.

I plan to.

I flip the medal over to see the back.

Grandma sweeps the hair off my forehead. "You know, your mom was your age when Grandpa died and this is bringing back some tough memories for her, but she wanted you to have his medal."

Yeah, Mom's been overly smothering lately, but I can't imagine losing her or Dad right now. I mean, Dad travels a lot, training people how to use computer software, but I know he's always coming home.

Mr. Madina pats my back. "You better start practicing that Mario game. Next time we play, I'm going to beat you." He gives me a hug.

He says this every time we play a game, but he's never once beaten Sam or me.

Before Sam leaves, he comes over to check out the medal. "We'll have to look this one up in the magazines to see what it's called and what it's given for."

He totally read my mind.

....

As I climb into bed, my thoughts blur. I'm still peeved that Kirk's captain, but I think about Grandpa, too. If Grandma's right, and he and I are alike, he'd agree with me that I should be leading the team and not Kirk. If I could blow the candles out all over again, I'd wish to run faster than anyone else against Palmetto and to secure a win for my team. I'd be a hero, for sure. Maybe Tuesday will be my day.

CHAPTER 2

SEPTEMBER 8, 2001
SATURDAY

....

Sam invited me to sleep over tonight, and Mom's going to drop me at his house around the corner on her way to run errands. Sam's next-door neighbor, Mrs. Wilkey, is lying flat on the ground near her flowers as we pass by. She's decked out in her usual long sleeve T-shirt, hat, and big sunglasses. We always joke that she's covering up the bite marks from her vampire husband. When we were little, Sam and I both believed the rumors about him lurking the neighborhood at night, sucking kids' blood. Everyone did.

Mom brakes suddenly, hops out of the car, and runs over to Mrs. Wilkey.

I grip the dashboard as Mom helps Mrs. Wilkey to her feet and eventually to the front door. Vampire or not, I hope Mom doesn't plan to go inside that creepy house.

Mrs. Wilkey grabs the knob and opens the door. Suddenly, a ghost-white arm reaches toward Mom. The arm wedges between her and Mrs. Wilkey and loops around Mrs. Wilkey's waist as Mom takes a step back. *Come on! Get out of there!* She stands still and the white hand is back. It grips the door, so pale it's practically see-through, even from here. Mom nods her head. I see her talk and then nod some more.

Finally, the hand closes the door and Mom comes back. "That poor family."

I stare at her. "Did you see Mr. Wilkey?"

"The poor lady's blood sugar probably dropped. A little juice should fix her right up."

"But did you see Mr. Wilkey?"

"Yes. I saw him. They're going to need you to help them around the yard till it gets cooler. Only two months or so."

Help them? No way.

Mom's still rambling. "She's getting too old for this heat . . ."

I have to go *there*?

". . . wants to keep the yard looking nice . . ."

I know he's not really a vampire, but *still*.

". . . feels like it's the least she can do for him since he had to give up his landscaping business. So after church tomorrow you can cut their grass. The lawn mower will be outside waiting for you."

"No. Come on, Mom, please. I'll wash the dishes for a month."

"What's wrong with you? It's just yard work. It certainly won't kill you."

"You don't even know them. Why'd you volunteer me?"

"She was lying on the *ground*. Was I supposed to drive right by? Maybe now they'll come out of their shells a little." Mom starts the car.

Sam and the Wilkeys live on the same corner with their houses facing different directions. From the garage, Mr. Madina waves to Mom as she pulls into the driveway. I climb out, still mad but thankful to get away from her before she signs me up for any more charity work at creepy old men's homes.

So far, there's only one other kid here—Kirk. Who the heck invited him?

I walk up the driveway and Sam tosses me a football. "My dad just ordered pizza. The rest of the guys should be here any sec."

I nod. I've got nothing to say to him if Kirk's here.

Sam gets me and says, "I saw Kirk at the store this morning. Thought he might want to come meet some eighth graders for once."

I force a smile. "Are Matt and Rigo coming?" They're not on our cross country team but they hang with Sam and me almost every day at school.

"They're on their way. So is Bobby. We should have enough to make two teams."

Great. We'll get to see if Kirk has some mad football skills, too.

Bobby Brinkmann and I used to play together a lot in kindergarten. I was at his house the day I busted my arm when I jumped out of his tree using a garbage bag as a parachute. Mom was crazy mad. Especially when I told her Bobby said it had worked for him before. We didn't see each other much after that. Sometimes his mom would call to invite me over, but we were always busy. Now we hang out to play football and basketball and stuff, but my parents don't really know about it.

Suddenly, we hear a crash in the garage as a pile of junk falls over. We rush to help Mr. Madina but he says, "No, it's okay. You boys go play, I can handle this mess. I tried to get my parents to get a storage space before they moved back overseas. But did they listen?" He laughs.

As we walk back to the front yard, Sam asks me, "What's wrong with you?"

For one, Kirk's here and you invited him; plus I have to work for the Wilkeys. "Nothing."

Sam throws me the ball and says, "Kirk wants us to practice with him tomorrow. We should do one more long run before the Palmetto meet anyway. You in?"

It'd give me a chance to try to keep up with Kirk and figure out what I have to do to beat him, but I can't go. I point toward the house on the corner. "I have to do yard work for the Wilkeys until the weather cools off. Starting tomorrow."

Sam freezes. "For real?"

Kirk smiles. "This may sound weird, but I like edging yards."

We stare at him. I knew there was something off with this kid.

"I do. I'll help you, Jake. Maybe we can run after."

Sam says, "You don't get it. It's for the Wilkeys. No one wants to go there."

Kirk shrugs. "Why not? Do they have something to do with Palmetto Ridge?"

We have a lot to fill him in on if he's going to hang with us. I shake my head. "Mr. Wilkey's just . . . creepy. People say he's a vampire, but we know that's only to scare the little kids in the neighborhood."

Kirk busts out laughing. "You're kidding, right?"

Sam and I look at each other. Then we sorta laugh.

I throw the ball to Sam. "People do say that, but it's not like we believe it. Still, he's weird. He never comes outside. And just now, I saw his arm—it's pure white. Like it's never seen the sun ever in its whole life . . . and we live in *Florida*! There's something odd about him."

Kirk points at Sam, then me. "You guys think he's a vampire and you say *he's* the weird one?" He cracks up.

Sam should never have invited Kirk.

Matt, Rigo, and Bobby drop their bikes on the sidewalk and walk over to us.

"What's so funny?" Rigo says.

Sam tosses the ball in the air. "Nothing. We were just filling Kirk in on Mr. Wilkey."

Kirk straightens and holds his side. It must hurt from all the laughing he's been doing. "Come on. You don't *all* believe it, do you?"

"No." Bobby grabs the ball from Sam. "It's just a legend. We used to joke about it, ya' know, to scare the little kids around here."

Kirk snatches the ball from Bobby. "You sure? I mean, if I just happened to walk over here," Kirk walks to the corner, "and I just happened to throw the ball in this guy's yard—"Kirk chucks the ball—"you're telling me you'd go get it?"

Bobby stares at him. Then he shrugs. "Of course, I would, but I bet Rigo wouldn't."

Rigo's eyes bug out. Everyone's staring, waiting to see what he'll do.

Bobby pushes Rigo. "Go get it. We've got a game to play."

Rigo hurries as fast as he can (there is a reason he's not on the cross country team) and hurls the ball at Kirk. "Better watch out. I'm ready to take your spot on the team."

We all laugh.

Sam says to Rigo, "We can use you on Tuesday for sure. Even if you don't run, you can stake out the woods and help us take down Tyler Montgomery."

Bobby picks his teeth with a pine needle. "Tyler from Palmetto?"

I jerk around to face him. "You know him?"

"He's on my travel basketball team. He thinks he's the best." Bobby scoffs.

Matt, who's also on the team, nods in agreement, as does Rigo, who has had his own run-ins with Tyler.

It's good to know other people think Tyler's a punk, too. He deserves what Sam and I have planned for him. When I tell Kirk about Tyler tripping me last year (but leaving out the pantsing incident), his mouth falls open, but Bobby, Matt, and Rigo don't seem surprised at all.

Sam then lays out our plan for this coming Tuesday. "We go early and stash a cup of water behind a tree. We need to stay in front of Tyler. Just as we pass the cup, we pull it out and toss it at his shorts."

Kirk shakes his head. "You'll get our whole team disqualified. No punk is worth that."

Easy for him to say. He wasn't the one on the ground last year with his underwear halfway down his legs.

Bobby raises his hand. "I'm not on the team, so I'll do it. No one will even know it's me. I can hide in the woods and wait for him to run by. I really can't stand that kid."

Maybe this is why Mom and Dad warned me to stay away from Bobby. He clearly loves trouble, but I'm glad he's offering to help us.

"You can't be serious. Right?" Kirk looks at me. Then at Sam. "Right?"

Neither of us says anything.

Bobby claps once. "That settles it. I'll mark it on my calendar. So, we playing football or not?"

We start to divide the teams as the pizza delivery guy shows up. At the same time, Bobby's dad drives by and Bobby goes stiff.

Mr. Brinkmann rolls down the window of his big truck and looks at him. "What are you doing here?"

Bobby looks around. He grabs the ball from Kirk's

hands. "I dropped my ball when I was riding home. I just stopped to pick it up."

Mr. Brinkmann's eyes narrow as he watches Mr. Madina fork out some cash to pay for the three pizzas. "Throw your bike in back and get in. Now."

Bobby moves double-time and is in the truck in seconds. He takes Sam's football with him. The truck's too high so I can't see inside, but I hear a smack, then a yelp, and the truck speeds off.

Bobby's always been a little bit of a punk, but his dad seems like a total jerk. I turn to Sam. "What about your ball?"

He shrugs. "It's no big deal. I'll get it later."

Rigo also has to leave to babysit his little sister, so Mr. Madina gives him five slices to go. The rest of us head inside. We eat in total silence and I can't help but feel bad for Bobby getting slapped by his dad in front of us all.

....

Captain Kirk, Matt, Sam, and I settle into bean bags in front of the TV in Sam's bedroom and he pulls out his Nintendo *Air Combat* game.

Kirk flips through the other games. "How about Madden?"

We look at him like he's crazy. "You don't like war games?"

He shrugs. "I'd just rather play Madden. I get enough military stuff at home. My dad's in the Navy."

"Really?" Sam and I say together.

"Yeah, but he's getting out in December. That's why we moved here. My parents are both from Coral Springs and they wanted to come home."

I sit up. "So is he on a ship or something?"

"Nah. He's in Washington, DC."

I didn't know there was a Navy base there. I'll have to look it up online later.

Matt hands Kirk a controller. "I bet you'll be happy when he's home for good."

Sam shows Kirk our stack of old war magazines. "Look at these."

Matt pops Madden into the Nintendo. He explains to Kirk, "These two are like war freaks or something."

Sam and I look at each other and shrug. He's got a point.

I pull the *LIFE* magazine Sam gave me for my birthday and the medal from my bag.

Sam grabs the medal. "This is so cool. We gotta remember to look it up."

Kirk scribbles out a competition chart with all our names. "Are we gonna play or what?"

Kirk's not as bad as I thought; I can see us hanging with him sometimes. I don't get how he's not interested in the magazines, though, or how he thinks I'm wrong for wanting to get back at Tyler, especially since Kirk's dad's in the military. Soldiers are trained to fight back—doesn't he know that?

I grab the game controller as Aamber and her best friend, pain-in-the-butt Katie, crash through the doorway and spray us with silly string.

Aamber's been doing this to me since we first met. She knows how much I hate it—it's like being stuck in a web.

We jump up and charge them, but the cans are already empty.

Sam holds his door handle. "Get out."

The girls crack up as they leave his room. "Got you good."

When they're gone Kirk says, "That's nothing. I've got sisters at home and I know a great way to get back at Aamber and Katie. Let's put Crisco on the toilet seat. When they use the bathroom, they'll slip into the bowl."

"Gross." Matt bumps Kirk's fist.

"Wait," I hold my hand up. "You think it's wrong that I want to get back at Tyler, but you think it's okay to get back at the girls?"

"There's a difference," Kirk says. "This is just for fun."

But I don't see the difference. Payback is payback. Still, Kirk's speed is going to help us beat Palmetto; his dad's in the Navy; he makes plans like Sam and me; *and* he has great prank ideas. I take it all back. Kirk can hang with us anytime.

We head for the kitchen. And then to the bathroom with a tub of Crisco in hand.

CHAPTER 3

SEPTEMBER 9, 2001
SUNDAY

....

Mom and Dad picked me up for church at the crack of dawn—they never let me skip for anything. I'm just glad Sam and Kirk both offered to help me at the Wilkeys' after Mass. As the three of us head over, I glance at the dark curtains hanging in the house's front window as we walk toward the porch. There's a lawn mower waiting. The edger's there, too, but there's no rake and no bag on the mower.

I push the mower to the middle of the lawn. "I guess we should just leave the grass once it's cut."

Kirk glances at the closed garage door. "I'm sure there's a rake somewhere. Do they have a shed out back?" He walks around the side of the house. We follow— knowing full well that there's a shed because we sometimes hear noises coming from it when we're in Sam's backyard.

The door to the shed's open and Kirk barges in. He walks back out with an empty jar and holds it to our faces. "I bet he uses this to store the extra blood he sucks."

Just when I was starting to like him, he has to go and say something stupid. "Ha ha! Did you find a rake or not?"

He disappears again and comes back with a pair of pliers. "And I bet he uses this to pluck out the eyeballs of his prey."

"Hilarious." I push past him, grab the rake, and walk to the front of the house.

It takes us about an hour to finish and the yard looks decent when we're done. I hope Sam will help me every week. Kirk, too, as long as he lays off the vampire comments.

At the bottom of the porch steps we spot three cold Gatorades. Sam and I look at each other, then at the house.

Kirk picks up all three. "You afraid to drink them or something?"

I reach for the green one. "Of course not."

Sam swipes the red one.

Kirk inspects the blue one that's left. He lifts it into the light and shakes it upside down. "You know, some-one could slip a really tiny needle with poison through this cap and you'd never see it." Then he laughs uncontrollably.

Seriously, one minute Kirk's great and the next he's making fun of us. I can't figure him out, and I hate when I can't figure things out.

....

I know we'll miss the beginning of the Eagles game if we do one last practice run, but nothing is more important than beating Palmetto on Tuesday, and besides, I'll make it back for the second half. Tuesday's a home meet for us, so Sam, Kirk, and I decide to run our own course to practice. Sam and I go slower than normal, looking for a location to leave the cup of water.

Kirk jogs back around. "You guys are too slow. I'll catch you later."

The frown he throws our way before leaving is a slap for sure. I wonder, though, if Tyler had pantsed Kirk if he wouldn't be doing the exact same thing that Sam and I are.

Deep down, I already know the answer, but I don't get it. I just don't.

Sam and I make it back home by halftime of the Eagles's game and Mom hands us warm cheesesteaks. Though I'm pumped, the Rams are up 14 to 3 at the start of the third. *Come on, Eagles.* They don't look good today.

Mom breaks out a cherry pie early in the fourth. It must be lucky because McNabb completes a pass to Cecil Martin and we score. Akers makes the field goal. Then, can you believe it? We do it again! Incredible.

We all whoop and chant, "Fly, Eagles, Fly!" But, apparently it doesn't help them keep their momentum because the birds lose when the Rams make a twenty-six-yard field goal. The Eagles have started their season 0–1. I seriously hope our cross country team does better.

CHAPTER 4
SEPTEMBER 10, 2001
MONDAY

....

Someone opens my blinds. *No, not yet. Five more minutes.*

Mom's hair spills forward as she leans in to give me a kiss. "Time to get up, honey."

I rub my eyes and stretch, then sloth out of bed. I throw my jersey on over a T-shirt for team pictures later.

In the kitchen, Dad's pouring coffee into his thermos. "Morning, champ."

I sit at the counter. Mom left me a plate of scrambled eggs and wheat toast. "You leaving today?"

"Right now, actually. I've got an early flight." He kisses the top of my head and walks toward the door. "Good luck tomorrow. I'm sorry I won't be there."

Me too, but I don't say it out loud; it'll only make him feel worse. I hate that he has to travel every week. His job

35

as a software trainer stinks because he never gets to see any of my meets or come to any events at school. I know he hates it, too. I down the food in four bites, grab my backpack and Eagles hat, and then head to Sam's house.

The street's buzzing with lawn mowers, neighbors jogging, and kids heading to school. Mrs. Wilkey's usually outside plucking at her garden. Not today, but her yard looks pretty great.

Aamber and Katie pass me on their bikes and pretend not to see me. Must be my lucky day. Before I'm totally clear of them, though, Aamber stops and turns to face me. "You wait, Jake. When you least expect it, we'll get you good."

"Sure you will." I laugh. "I forgot to ask, how was that toilet water? Nice and refreshing?"

They scowl at me before quickly taking off. The two of them go everywhere together. They even do our announcements on MMS TV at school every morning. And student council. And yearbook. And a few other clubs at Mangrove Middle School. I'd hurl if I had to do morning announcements on TV—I hate speaking in front of people. Sam and I just stick to running.

Sam hops off his front porch swing when he sees me. He takes a bite of a muffin and mumbles, "So, Kirk's pretty cool, right?"

I shrug. "I guess, but that captain band will be mine."

"I'm sure it will. It's a good thing Bobby's going to deal with Tyler so we can focus on running. And winning." Sam takes off. "Come on. We're late."

I dart after him.

At the intersection across from school, we catch our breath as George, the crossing guard, blows his whistle and steps into the road. Sam sticks out his hand the way he has every day since first grade and George shakes it as we jog past him.

We reach the park behind the school and Rigo's already shooting hoops. He always walks his sister to her school then hangs out here playing ball till we show up.

Matt looks up from his math book. "It's 8:54. How are we supposed to get a game in if you two are late?"

Sam points at me. "His fault." He turns back to Matt and Rigo.

Rigo tosses Sam the basketball. "How about a game after school instead?"

"Can't," Sam says. "We have team pictures."

The bell rings and we walk toward the building.

Matt grabs me around the neck and tries to trip me. "Right, cross country. What a lame sport."

He's Mangrove's star basketball player, but running up and down a small court's nothing. I hop over Matt's leg and wrangle free of his grip. "The only way you'd run is if someone dangled your teddy bear in front of you."

Sam and Rigo crack up.

Matt smacks me on the back. "Teddy bear? That's the best you can come up with?" He takes off and we dart after him.

....

Matt fumbles to a stop outside the social studies door and the rest of us slam into him. Mrs. Cruz, who's new to Mangrove this year, steps out of the way just before we flatten her against the wall. "Morning, boys."

We all apologize and then scramble for our seats. Mrs. Cruz is kind of weird. She talks to every kid who walks in the door. She stares us right in the eyes and nods a lot when we answer questions. And her room— it's covered from top to bottom with dream-big-do-the-right-thing-save-the-earth-don't-step-on-the-ants-type posters. She says she's going to teach us to change the world, but I'm not sure how we can change the world if we're stuck following rules. And she's big on rules.

I whip out my journal and copy down the question of the day that's posted on the board. *Big Mac or Whopper?* I so don't get Mrs. Cruz's logic. What does this have to do with social studies? And how can I possibly write three paragraphs about why the Whopper is better? It just is.

Mrs. Cruz clicks the TV on to the MMS station, then

takes attendance. In a minute, Aamber and Katie will be smiling on screen. They'll be fluffing and twirling their matching brown hair as they scream what a great day it is at Mangrove Middle.

Bobby waves his arm around in the air and squirms wildly in his seat. He's got a faded bruise on his cheek.

"You okay?"

"Of course." He brushes off the whole thing.

Finally, Mrs. Cruz sees him and sighs. "Yes, Bobby?" We've only been in school for eleven days, but she already *gets* him.

He wiggles like a little kid. "Can I pretty please go to the bathroom?"

She doesn't even look up from her attendance sheet. "No."

He laughs. No one else does. It's hard to feel bad for him when he acts like a jerk.

....

At practice, I'm sandwiched between Sam and Kirk for the team picture. Their white captain armbands stick out against our blue uniforms. I *will* run my fastest tomorrow. I *will* win this for our team. Coach will *have* to make me captain, too.

We smile.

Click.

Sam and I line up to practice our starts and sprints—an easy day before our big match. Kirk's hanging with us, not the seventh graders, and gives me a great starting line pointer. It's like he's good at everything. Really good. We're finally ready to take down the six-time county champs, Palmetto Ridge. And Tyler Montgomery. Less than twenty-four hours to go.

Coach hollers over our chatter. "Great practice, boys. Bring everything you've got tomorrow. It's the most important meet of our regular season. Cedar Cove only rostered three runners, but Palmetto Ridge, well, you know in the past that they haven't always played fair. Just run like you've been trained to. Keep it clean. No matter what happens, you'll be able to hold your head up high. If you beat Palmetto, you should be sitting pretty till county finals."

Kirk looks at Sam and me. I turn away. I'm not going to back down from my plan. But my heart is racing, like I've just finished a long run.

It's time to conquer the one team we've never been able to beat.

Tomorrow, victory will be ours.

CHAPTER 5

September 11, 2001
Tuesday

....

Mom kisses my forehead. "Rise and shine."

I pull up the covers.

She yanks them off. "Come on. Breakfast is hot. I'll see you after school. Run hard. Promise?"

"Yeah." I'm glad she'll be there. She's not only going to see my best race yet, but I'll also get to listen to her all the way home talk about how sorry she feels for "that boy who wet his pants."

I get dressed, pack my sneakers and running shorts in a bag, then shove them in my backpack. Last week, I would have sworn that today I'd be packing the captain armband, too—instead, Kirk is. At least I have Grandpa's medal. I wish he could see me run. I take the medal from my dresser for luck.

In an instant, my stomach lurches. I haven't learned anything. My plan is all offensive strategy. What if Tyler's planning something for me again? Stupid, stupid, stupid. My throat's tight as I clench the medal in my fist.

I skip breakfast and rush to Sam's. The sun's already blaring and the street's busy as usual with school buses, joggers, and kids.

Sam bounces down the steps of his porch and I toss my football to him. He lets it fall as he yanks off the headphones of his Walkman. "Whoa, give me a sec, would ya?"

I pick up the ball and frown. "You gotta always be prepared."

"What going on with you?" He grabs the ball from my hands.

"Prepared. We're not fully prepared. What if Tyler's planning something for me today? Or for you?"

"Chill. One of us can stay in front of him and one of us right behind him. We'll watch him the whole time. Go long." He throws a deep pass.

But if I stay behind Tyler, I won't win the race. Nothing's going right. I sprint ahead and the ball bobbles in my hands. "Yeah, but we need to make sure he doesn't have someone else helping him."

"No way. Today, the Bugs won't even know what hit them."

He's right about that. Palmetto doesn't know about Kirk. Tyler won't be expecting Bobby. And me, I just need to stay focused and run. I need to beat Tyler—and Kirk.

....

We get to the park a little early but Matt and Rigo are already waiting for us at the basketball court with Kirk and Bobby.

Matt swishes a three pointer. "Hurry up. We've only got ten minutes."

Bobby, Rigo, and Matt team up against the three of us. Five minutes in, they're winning 8–2.

I charge Bobby and make a lay-up.

He shoves me. "What'd you do that for?"

Sam jumps between us. "Chill. It's part of the game."

I stare Bobby down till he backs off and covers the whole thing with a laugh.

The warning bell rings. I take a quick shot then grab my stuff. "You guys coming to watch the race?" I'm hoping Bobby won't back out.

Bobby slaps my palm. "Heck yeah."

I can't wait to see Tyler's face at the finish line. If he even finishes.

Matt says, "You better squash those Bugs."

"That's the plan," I holler as we dart toward the school.

Kirk heads down the hall for math as the rest of us run toward social studies class.

Mrs. Cruz stops us inside the doorway. "Morning, boys."

Once in my seat, I flip open my journal and write the question of the day: *What if cows made root beer instead of milk?* What planet is this teacher from? Cows make milk; it's just what they do.

The TV's on our MMS station. I hope Katie and Aamber will announce the meet; we could use some more fans, but they'll probably skip it just because of Sam and me. Payback.

Bobby's messing around as usual while Mrs. Cruz takes attendance. She gives him a warning.

I read the question on the board, again. Cows . . . milk . . . root beer. I tap my pencil on my forehead and try to see what Sam's scribbling on his paper next to me. He's got two paragraphs written already, but it only takes one line to say how *impossible* it is.

I'm about to put my head down and skip the assignment when Aamber and Katie come back to class, even though the announcements haven't started.

Then I notice Principal Ogden standing in the doorway—his face wearing a concerned look—as he motions Mrs. Cruz into the hall.

I watch her through the skinny door window as he speaks with her and she covers her mouth with her hand.

A few minutes later, she comes back in and her dark skin looks pale. She closes her eyes and inhales. When she opens them again, she glances around the room. I watch to see if she's looking at anyone in particular. Maybe someone's mom or dad got in an accident and she's gonna have to break the news. But she keeps looking around—at all of us. I get a little creeped out.

She looks like she's about to fall apart and quickly faces the board for a few seconds. When she turns back around, she straightens her jacket and tells us to open our books and read, but she never gives us a page number to start on. She walks slowly toward the connecting classroom. As she grabs for the handle, Mr. Grier comes through the door. She stumbles and he barely catches her. It's a little freaky to see her like this. Even Katie, who's always running her mouth, is quiet.

The TV in the adjoining room is blaring: "I repeat, two planes have hit the World Trade Towers." The reporter's almost screaming.

Mrs. Cruz looks like she might hurl. Mr. Grier helps her to a chair and then goes back to his own room. Matt switches our TV to a news channel. All eyes dart to a picture of a silver plane in a perfect blue sky. The sun is shining on it. And then, *BAM!* The plane disappears into the side of a tall building. Big smoke balls mixed with flames roll out. Gasps echo through the classroom.

Bobby laughs and slaps Rigo on the shoulder. "Cool."

Yeah, those must be some wicked special effects. Except Mrs. Cruz is whiter than my blank journal paper. And the reporter is still shouting. Two planes. New York City. Two towers. Accident?

I turn back to the TV. The blue sky is now black.

Our room is silent except for the reporter. It's pretty obvious this isn't a movie, but it's a pretty big accident. I look at Sam. His eyes are wide and he looks shocked. Maybe even scared.

I lean over to him. "What's going on?"

"I don't know." He breathes all heavy. "Maybe the autopilot was set wrong. Sometimes captains use that when they have to go to the bathroom."

That makes sense because if the pilots had been in their seats, they would have definitely seen the gigantic building in front of them. But the reporter said something about two planes. That means two different sets of pilots. How could they both have made the same mistake?

From behind me, I hear a half-laugh. "Someone's

getting fired for sure. The air traffic controller must have been sleeping or something."

I look back to the TV. The images of the plane hitting the building plays again. And again. As much as I want someone to turn it off, I can't peel my eyes away. The plane. The silver plane. Dad flies in one every week. But he flew yesterday. Not today. He was flying to Raleigh and staying there till Thursday. Right? I try to remember his schedule. He always writes it out and posts it on the fridge for us. I didn't look at it yesterday or today. I've been so obsessed with the Palmetto meet. *Please, please let him be on the ground.*

"No. No!" Someone yells, "Turn it off."

Mrs. Cruz's staring at the TV, but I don't think she's really watching. She looks more like she's zoning out. Katie gets up and turns the TV off and shakes Mrs. Cruz back to reality. She snaps out of it but then starts pacing. Mr. Grier motions for her to go into the hallway. She turns to us before she heads out and says, "Just read, or go back to your journals. Something. I'll be right back."

No one does anything, though. Bobby says we're being attacked, but he just wants to get everyone freaked out, like always. It must have been an accident. Our country could never be under attack. Just like cows could never make root beer.

....

Several people jump in their seats when the intercom suddenly blares. "Mrs. Cruz, please excuse the interruption," a voice calls over the P.A. "Could you send the following students to the front office? Andrew Drum, Bridget Fitzpatrick, Blake Stopher, and Jacqui VanKamp. Their parents are here to pick them up. Tell them to bring their things."

I doubt they're all going to the dentist.

"Also," the intercom blares once more, "I need Jake Green."

I'm frozen at my desk.

Sam knows Mom doesn't believe in letting me miss school for anything, so this can't be good.

"Think your mom has inside information about this?" Sam asks me. "Is she picking you up because your Uncle Hugh knows something?"

I hope that's all it is, but I'm afraid to go to the office because I think I'll crumble if any of this has to do with Dad. Before I close my backpack, I reach for Grandpa's medal. For some reason, it makes me feel a little better.

I head to the office. There are about twenty kids being signed out. When I turn the corner, Mom rushes at me and throws her arms around my neck. Other parents are doing the same with their kids.

Mom hurries me toward the front door, and I feel her shaking.

"What's going on? Is Dad okay?"

"I don't know. I mean, yes. Well, he should be. He's in Raleigh, but I haven't heard from him. I don't know what's happening but there's something going on."

Mom's more wired than I am after eating a full bag of Skittles. She's freaking me out. "You mean with the planes? Can't we call Dad?"

"You know about the planes?" She hugs me again. "I've been trying to call Dad, but I can't reach him on his cell. When we get home, we'll try to find the hotel's number."

I climb in the front seat. "It was just an accident, right?" My gut knows it wasn't, but I sure wish someone would say it's one big mistake.

She looks at me for a few seconds. "Yeah, I'm sure it was."

She's more transparent than a ghost. Always has been. Usually I like that about her. It makes it easy for me to figure her out. But now it makes me scared. I wish Dad would answer his phone. I need to know he's okay.

....

Mom pulls into the garage and closes the door before she

even shuts off the car. I bolt out of the passenger side and race for the refrigerator to find Dad's schedule. I don't need to read it though, because Mom's right behind me and her cell phone's already ringing. I know it's him. I know it.

Tears sting my eyes as I wrap my hand around the medal in my pocket. Mom hits the speaker button so I can hear, too. I think we're all stuck in the moment because no one says anything for a few seconds, though we're all breathing a sigh of relief.

Mom breaks the silence first. "Dan, are you okay?"

"I'm fine. Shocked by all this, but okay. How about you two?"

"We need you to come home. Today. Don't fly."

Mom's commanding tone surprises me. She is always the one reminding me that we shouldn't pressure Dad or make him feel bad for being away so much.

"I'm already at a rental car place. I'll be there in about twelve hours. Right now they don't have a car available, but they're bringing one from another lot."

He can't see Mom shaking her head so I say, "Okay, Dad." His calmness makes me feel so much better. "Can you check in with us every few hours?"

"I'll do my best, champ. I don't know how long my phone battery will hold out. I love you, and I'll see you soon."

"Love you, too."

Mom takes the phone from me, turns off the speaker, and walks into the other room to talk to Dad privately.

I turn on the TV in the kitchen and hear a reporter say that a plane hit the Pentagon a few minutes ago and there are reports that other planes might be missing. These are definitely not accidents. The pilots have to have been working together. Sam and I both know that every mission has a purpose. I think back to all I've read about Pearl Harbor and this is a little bit like that—only our own planes were used this time. All I can think about is how many others might crash today.

Mom's returned to the kitchen, her eyes glazed over as she stares at the TV. "Good, Lord." She shudders and then rushes around the kitchen until she produces eight flashlights and two hurricane lanterns. She grabs her purse and keys. "Let's go."

"Where?"

"We need to get to the store."

"Now?" I follow her out to the garage.

"Yes," she says. "We need to get supplies."

For someone who's always avoided my military talk, she sounds an awful lot like she's planning for combat. And as much as I've always wanted a real mission, I have no idea what's coming next and that freaks me out.

Outside the grocery store, Mom grabs a cart and tells

me to get one, too. As we pass through the front doors, I see a crowd crammed around the lotto desk. Everyone's staring at something. Screams mix with sobs and a few people mumble "Oh, my God!"

Someone cries, "It's gone!"

I stand on the bottom rail of the cart to see over their heads and spot a TV screen. Instead of the black smoke that's been trailing out of the two tall buildings all morning, there are now puffs of smoke and only one of the two buildings hit in New York City is left standing. I glance back at Mom, but her face is hidden behind her hands. She's sobbing. I jump off the cart and head toward her.

She straightens and sniffles. "Come on. We need to hurry."

I look around. No one else seems to be in a hurry. Instead, people are hugging each other. Some stand with eyes wide and hands covering their mouths. One lady is praying her rosary beads and kisses the cross at the end. I can't believe the building fell—it was massive. I really hope everyone inside made it out.

Mom grabs my cart and forces me forward. She darts straight for the laundry aisle. She piles containers of bleach into her basket, which makes sense for a hurricane, but not this, I don't think. Next come candles. Mom grabs about twenty of them. She hits up the batteries, the canned food, toilet paper, and finally the bottled water. Both our carts are overflowing and I can't help but think that this stash will last us at least a year. I drop a few boxes of Cheez-Its and brownie mix into my basket, too—just in case.

A few other shoppers have crammed carts, too. They must all think more is going to happen today. Or soon.

When we go to pay, the cashier isn't even at the register. She's glued to the TV at the lotto counter.

Mom waves her arms at her. "Excuse me!"

Finally, the girl comes over, wiping her wet eyes on her uniform shirt. "I just can't believe it," she repeats, over and over.

Normally Mom would have wrapped her arms around the girl and told her everything would be okay. But not today. She just pays the bill and drags me quickly out of the store, our full carts bumping along with us.

The heat hits me as the double doors open. "Why are we in such a rush?" I finally say.

"We need to get home. It's just safer."

She stops at the ATM and withdraws money. Then, on our way home, we drive through our bank's ATM line and she takes out even more cash.

"Why do you need all that?" I ask.

She shoves the stash of bills in her purse and

drives off. "You just never know. You have to always be prepared."

"For what?"

"Life, Jake. For life. For things you can't control."

Suddenly I see Mom in a whole new light. She's a much better soldier than either Sam or me. She prepares for all the just-in-cases. I hope that's all this is. A just-in-case. I look at her and can't help but wonder how long she's been expecting an attack like this to happen to us. It's like she's going through a well-thought-out checklist in her head.

Mom doesn't speak the rest of the way home, but when I look over and see a tear fall down her cheek, she actually says a lot. I wish Dad would hurry up and get home.

....

At four o'clock, Dad called again. He'd just gotten a car and was leaving Raleigh. I wish he'd left when we first talked to him that morning because he'd be half-way home by now. Mom's on the phone with Grandma and is really upset. It's obvious she's is refusing to come stay with us. Mom claims she needs to keep an eye on Grandma, but it sounds more like Mom *needs* Grandma or like she needs us all in one place. She hasn't let me out of her sight all day. It stinks because I want to watch the news, but every time I try, she cries and shuts it off. I try to call Sam so he can fill me in on what's going on, but no one answers at his house, which is strange because even if his parents left him at school, he'd be home by now. I assume the cross country meet was canceled and realize it's the first time I've thought about that all day.

I wish we could wind the clock backward and undo today completely, kind of like when you reboot a video game. Start over and be more prepared, like Mom— unlike me, or the people on those planes and in those buildings, for that matter. Too bad there are no do-overs in real life.

....

The doorbell catches me off guard and I jump.

When I open the door, Sam hands me a plate of brownies and says, "From my mom." Mrs. Madina bakes all the time, especially when she's upset. I can picture her banging around the kitchen to avoid the news. I guess she's like Mom in that way.

Mr. Madina pats my shoulder as he passes through the doorway. "I know your dad is out of town so we came to see if you guys need anything."

I point at Mom. She's sitting at the computer reading only the updates she wants and avoiding the rest of the news. Mr. Madina goes over to her and gives her a big hug. She breaks down crying in his arms. She's gone from being so put together and in control to a mess in only a few hours.

Sam and I head to my room.

He sits on my bed. "Is your Dad okay?"

"Yeah, he rented a car. He's on his way home."

"That's good. You looked off the chain when you left school today."

"Has anything else happened since the plane hit the Pentagon? Mom's been so freaked out that I've kept the TV off."

"They're definitely saying that our country's being attacked. Both towers fell in New York and one more plane crashed in a field in Pennsylvania. They've stopped all flights and any that were still in the air were supposed to land at the closest airport. I guess they're trying to see how many planes don't respond."

That's when I realize that the planes, which usually fly overhead on their flight pattern to Ft. Lauderdale airport, have been eerily silent.

"So, how many haven't responded?"

"They didn't say, but some think that the people on board the fourth plane knew about the other attacks so they ambushed the hijackers and crashed the plane into the ground."

"For real?" I let it soak in. I think if I'd known I was going to die anyway I'd probably have done the same thing. "Those people are heroes."

"For sure."

Mr. Madina calls from the other room. "Sam?"

"Coming."

I walk him back toward the front door. "Is your family okay?"

"We're good. My mom wants us to stay home from school tomorrow, though. Just in case."

Sam heads outside, but his "just-in-case" stays with me. As I watch Sam and his dad leave, I start thinking about what will happen next. I'm sure the president's preparing for war right now, so we're going to be safe. I guess Kirk's dad won't get out in December, but I bet he'll be happy to defend our country after what happened today.

....

Mom finally falls asleep on the couch and I slip past her into the kitchen. I turn the TV on and hear that President Bush will be speaking in ten minutes. I lower the volume. *Please don't let her wake up until after I hear what the president says.* The reporter says based on "new and specific" information, officials think that some guy named Osama bin Laden from Saudi Arabia is to blame. They show a map on TV of the Middle East. It's so far away from here. A sense of relief, knowing that US pilots didn't do this, washes over me. But how did people from another country get control of our planes?

President Bush finally appears. He's so charged with energy, I can almost feel him through the screen. He talks about finding those responsible for the attacks and bringing them to justice. *What does he mean by that?* He asks us to unite in our resolve for justice and peace. He says that America has stood down enemies before and will do it again. Does he mean we'll retaliate? "We go forward to defend our freedom . . ." the president says and I almost let out a cheer. That's exactly right. We have to defend our country. I take Grandpa's medal from my pocket and palm it in my hand. We have to make someone pay for all this.

CHAPTER 6
SEPTEMBER 12, 2001
WEDNESDAY

....

Someone shakes me and I open my eyes.

"Dad!" I throw my arms around his neck.

"Hi, champ." He pulls me up from the recliner in the living room. "It's the middle of the night. You should go to your room and get some sleep."

"I'm glad you're home." I hug him one more time before heading to bed, knowing I'll sleep better now.

When I wake up, it's a little after noon and I come to the conclusion that Mom and Dad are letting me miss school. In the kitchen, I grab a bowl of cereal and pass Mom, who is sitting at the computer, on my way to the living room. She's got the Army-Navy store website up, which is odd because I haven't been a boy scout for years. I hear the TV on in my parents' room and go sit on the bed next to Dad. Live images of firemen in New York flash across the screen. They look like the miniature army men Sam and I used to play with, but they're climbing mountains of white, crumbled building parts. They wear masks over their faces, and the debris is still smoking even though it's been over a day since the buildings fell down. Writing in the corner of the TV reads AMERICA UNDER ATTACK. More words scroll across the bottom stating that the death toll's "expected to be in the thousands." *Thousands?* That's more than the number of kids at my school.

A reporter comes on the screen. Behind her, hundreds of people walk by. Some look out of it. Others seem determined, holding pictures in their hands. A little girl holds a poster with a picture on it that reads, "Daddy, where are you?" I hope her dad isn't one of the thousands who died. I wait for the reporter to tell me that some people survived. I wait some more, but all the news shows is the firemen picking through big piles of white stuff. And more faces, searching.

....

This afternoon, Dad made me turn off the TV after watching for only an hour, even though he kept sneaking off to watch it himself. I didn't need a break, even if some of it *was* hard to watch. It was better than sitting around, like I ended up doing the rest of the day. We had dinner; I finally talked to Sam on the phone, if only for a second, and I played Nerf hoops in my room. By that night, I decided I'd rather run cross country than sit at home like this.

Mom went to bed and Dad makes me a cup of hot chocolate.

I sit at the table. "How come Mom's acting so weird?"

"It's the attacks. They've got her rattled."

I stir in marshmallows. "Yeah, but she's so out of it and cries a lot."

He sits across from me with his own steaming mug. "Everyone handles things like this differently. These attacks have triggered something in her, and she's scared."

I take a sip. "Why do you think we were attacked like that?"

He shakes his head. "I'm not sure anyone will ever be able to answer that."

"Someone has to. Someone *must* know."

Dad's face turns serious looking. "You don't need to worry. We're okay here. The worst is over."

I'm not scared like Mom is. Not really. We were caught off guard yesterday, but President Bush says our military's prepared to fight back. I only wish Sam and I were old enough to enlist, because we'd help take down whoever did this.

CHAPTER 7

SEPTEMBER 13, 2001
THURSDAY

....

Mom brushes my cheek to wake me and then sits on my bed. She looks worried, and tired.

"I have to go back to work. Uncle Hugh needs me there. Dad's going to drop you off at school. If I can leave early to pick you up after, I will. If not, he'll get you."

"What about practice?"

"No. I want you to come right home." She stands, her head shaking in small, quick motions. "Besides it's supposed to rain all day."

"Come on. I need to practice." I'll never catch up to Kirk without it.

Her face tightens. "I said *no*."

She sighs and looks like she might say something else

but doesn't. After a few seconds, she kisses me goodbye, but I don't kiss her back.

Dad flips off the TV as I walk into the kitchen.

I scan the counters and table hoping Mom at least left breakfast. She didn't.

"Did they find anything else out yet?" I ask.

Dad offers me a box of granola bars. "No, they're still just looking for survivors."

"It's really okay if I walk to school. Sam will be waiting for me."

Dad's eyes are puffy underneath and he looks more like he's ready for bed—not like he just got up. "There's a nasty storm brewing off the coast."

I look out the window. It's gray, but not raining. "It's clear for now," I tell him.

"I don't think it's a good idea."

"Why not? I walk by myself all the time."

He studies my face. "I don't know. Your mom—"

"You even said the attacks are over. I'll be fine."

He lets out a long breath. "I know you will." He smothers me with a hug. "Be careful. And don't tell your mother. No need to stress her out any more than she is."

I grab my backpack, Eagle's hat, and football and head out the door to Sam's.

It's dead quiet outside. The clouds are swelling, and Dad was right—it's going to rain for sure. Other than a school bus, the roads seem abandoned. Up and down the street, American flags salute me from every house— except my own. None of them were flying two days ago.

The flag hanging near Sam's garage door brushes the top of my head as I jog up his porch steps, hoping he's waited for me. The front door swings open and Sam bursts through, but Mrs. Madina quickly pulls him back and kisses him goodbye. Then she hugs him for a solid ten seconds. He rolls his eyes and finally breaks free of her grip.

I wave to her as we run down the front walkway.

Mrs. Madina hugs Aamber, then yells, "Sam, wait for your sister!"

Before I can even ask, he says, "It's the only way she'll let us walk to school by ourselves." He fumbles with the newspaper in his hands.

Aamber sticks the last bite a Pop-Tart in her mouth and I laugh to myself because her shirt says PEACE, LOVE, AND POP-TARTS.

I talk louder as I run backward ahead of Sam, ready to chuck him a long pass. "These attacks are so messed up. Think we'll go to war? I wish I was old enough to enlist."

Aamber looks at me like I'm from another planet. "Are you kidding? Is that all you can think about right now? Did you actually *see* what happened? Didn't you see the towers fall? This isn't one of your video games. It's real life—and it's awful."

Something in the way she says that makes me feel like an idiot. I stop dead in my tracks. "I know it's real, but someone attacked us and we need to fight back. We're just defending ourselves."

"You're out of your mind. Nothing's going to get better if everyone keeps fighting all the time." She sounds like Kirk.

"Nothing's going to get better if we let them get away with it," I say back.

"Forget her." Sam holds up a newspaper. "Look at this. That fourth plane that went down in Pennsylvania, well, they still don't know where it was gonna hit, but I heard on TV some people think our own government shot it down before it could get to DC."

"Would the government really do that?"

He snatches the football from my hands. "Maybe. Can't blame them, right? As bad as it was, those people were going to die no matter what and the government could have saved a lot of other people by downing it."

"Maybe, but I can't imagine being the one that had to kill a bunch of innocent people."

Sam points to an article, PHONE CALLS PAINT PICTURE OF HEROISM IN THE SKY. I take the paper from him and read about three passengers who called their families to say there were men taking over the plane. One guy told his wife he was on a hijacked plane and when she asked if he was okay, he said no, but they were going to do something about it. A shiver jostles me despite the heat outside. If Dad had called me to say he was on one of those planes, well, I'd like to think I'd be strong, but I think I'd crumble instead. But if I was on the plane, I'm pretty sure I'd help the other passengers in their fight to take down the bad guys. I'm sure I would. Sam, too. Even if what Sam heard about our government shooting down the plane turns out to be true, these phone calls prove those people were heroes.

I scan the rest of the newspaper. So much has happened that I didn't even know about.

Finally I ask Sam, "Can I keep this?" We don't get the paper because Mom says it's all sad news.

"Yeah." Sam tosses the ball. "I still can't believe one of the terrorist pilots lived here in Coral Springs."

I do a one-eighty as we approach the intersection across from school. "I thought the pilots weren't American." The ball drops to my feet.

"Just because they lived here doesn't mean they were citizens."

True, but the US is huge. Our town's so small. "Why would he pick here?"

Sam picks up the ball and shakes George's hand as we cross the street. A light rain begins to fall. "You know how my dad works at the bank? Well, Mohamed Atta—the terrorist who lived here—had an account there. My dad remembers helping him."

My head's suddenly mixed up. I'm trying to understand everything Sam's telling me.

Aamber ditches us in front of the school. Once she's gone, Sam turns to me. "I wonder if we've ever seen the guy around, maybe at a restaurant or something. What if . . ." Sam shakes his head. "Never mind. It's just all so messed up."

"What if what?" I ask. "What if he lived next door? What if there are more guys still here?"

"Yeah, all of that. I can't believe someone that bad was living right here."

My stomach tightens and I think I might hurl.

We walk the rest of the way to the park behind school in silence and wait for Rigo and Matt. They're late and the park is eerily empty. The few kids who are around are caged inside the school fence; the gate is closed and locked. It definitely wouldn't stop some terrorist from getting into our school, but I guess the principal can't sit around and do nothing.

"Looks like we're on lockdown again," Sam says. "They did this after the attacks on Tuesday but you were already gone. We'll have to go to the front of the school to get in." Sam leans on the basketball pole. "Think we'll have practice later?"

I look at the thick clouds that are still forming. My brain's on overload. I'm kind of happy Mom's making me go right home, because I don't think I could run today even if I wanted to. "I'm not allowed to go either way."

"I hope we do. I don't want to be stuck in my house again."

Rigo rounds the corner and heads our way.

Sam tosses him the ball. "Hey. What's up?"

Rigo watches as the ball falls at his feet. He starts to say something, then stops. He looks at Sam, then at me, then back at Sam. He shakes his head and shuffles toward the school fence where Matt's already waiting. I'm just about to yell to Rigo, asking him what his problem is, when I hear a thud behind me. When I turn around, Sam is face down on the basketball court. Blood's pooling around his face.

Bobby stands over him. "Go back where you came from, O-sam-a!"

A small audience of kids trickle into the park.

I get in Bobby's face. "What's your problem?"

He steps back and looks at the crowd. No one moves.

I reach for Sam's arm and pull him up. His nose spews blood. "Come on, let's go to the nurse's office."

"Not here, you won't!" Bobby stands firm. Some kids stand with him, blocking our path to the school and forming an impassable front. Others hang back, but keep watching. I scan the faces in the crowd. What is going on?

Sam hunches over as he pinches his nose.

I try to push a couple of kids aside. "Come on. Sam needs to see the nurse."

But the barricade tightens with more kids, including Rigo. Matt climbs up on the fence. Of course he'll come help us.

I look back at Bobby and scream, "Get out of the way!" I grab Sam by the shirt and snake my way through the slew of kids, but Sam frees himself of my grip and takes off running. Kids surround me. I can't see Sam anymore. I shove people out of my way, but the circle's tightening in around me.

"That's right," Bobby yells after Sam. "Go home and pack your bags. Take your diaper-head dad and the rest of your family and get out of here." Bobby spins toward me and adds, "You too, traitor. Go home!"

My fist instantly makes contact with Bobby's eye. He stumbles backward off the court and I lunge at him again. I land on top of him and take another swing at his face.

Kids chant, "Fight, fight, fight!"

We wrestle in the growing puddles. Bobby claws at me and rips my shirt. Gripping my shoulders, he flips me onto my back and knocks the wind out of me. My head slams onto the ground, sending sprays of water into my eyes. I land a blind punch before he yanks my wrist and pummels me in the chest with his free hand, over and over. I chuck my knee upward and nail a good one right between his legs. He winces in pain, then rolls off me.

The rain picks up just as the warning bell blares. Kids scatter. I manage to get to my knees. Rigo's standing there, but he doesn't offer to help me up. Instead, he reaches for Bobby and drags him to class. Matt hops off the fence and heads toward the school without a word. What the heck's going on?

Sam's long gone. I'm alone, panting and confused. Nothing makes sense. I don't know what to do. Or where to go. Then I see it. A path of blood, splattered by rain, leading toward the intersection.

....

I sprint to Sam's house. The scene at the basketball court replays in my head, but it doesn't make sense. I ring the Madinas' doorbell, rain dripping from my soaked clothes.

Mrs. Madina peeks from behind the orange curtain. The chain catches as she opens the door. "I'm sorry, but Sam can't see you right now."

"Is he okay?"

Her soggy eyes freak me out a little. "His dad's cleaning him up, but I think it's going to be a long time before any of us will be okay again. I'll tell him you stopped by. You should get back to school, Jake."

"Can you tell him I'll call him later?"

She looks at me like she's finally seeing me. "Are you okay? You're a mess, too."

My shirt's ripped, but luckily Mrs. Madina can't see the throbbing in my head or chest. "I'm fine."

She looks my face over again. "I'll have him call you when he's up to it. He'll be fine. Don't you worry."

"But—"

"You're a good friend, Jake. But right now, Sam needs to stick close to home."

"Can—"

"I'll tell him you came by." Mrs. Madina seals the door between us.

....

The name *Osama* runs through my head. Bobby basically just accused Sam of being a terrorist. *Forget school.* I head home. The thought of Sam on the ground replays in my mind. My legs pick up pace. Images of blood pouring out of Sam's nose sweep through me. Our friends just stood there and watched. But what about Kirk? Was he there, too? I don't remember seeing him. *Think.* My legs are on auto and I'm running. Fast. Hard. The back of my head is pounding, but, still, I'd set a state record if anyone were timing me.

....

I rip my wet shirt off on the porch and inside I expect to have to explain to Dad why I'm home. But he's MIA. I sign on to the Internet to look up *Osama.* A bunch of articles pop up and I click on the one that reads: TERRORISTS HAD TIES TO SOUTH FLORIDA AND OSAMA BIN LADEN. The first line reads: *Mohamed Atta, the leader of the American Airlines Flight 11 hijacking, moved to Coral Springs in April of 2001.*

The hairs on my arms and neck pop up.

I scroll down. A picture of a man with a towel on his head is wedged between some of the writing on the screen. I've never seen a real person wear this—only in history books. *Diaper-head* pops into my brain. That's what

Bobby called Sam's dad, but I've never seen Mr. Madina wear one of those.

I keep reading. Atta may have had connections with al-Qaeda and Osama bin Laden. But so far al-Qaeda hasn't claimed responsibility for the attacks. None of this has anything to do with Sam. Bobby's crazy, that's all. He needs to go see someone that will screw his head back on right—or maybe my fist was enough.

....

Dad comes in from the garage as I grab an ice pack from the freezer.

I hold it up to the back of my head. "Where were you? I came home to talk to you."

He rushes toward me and inspects the growing lump. "I was returning the rental car. What happened?"

"It's nothing."

The ringing phone interrupts us.

I wait for Dad to finish his conversation in order to explain this whole Bobby thing, but when he gets off the phone, he's steaming.

"That was the school." He folds his arms over his chest. "More specifically, Officer Roth."

"Good. So, is Bobby going to get suspended?"

"Bobby? They told me you punched him. I have to bring you in."

I set the ice pack down. "I did punch him, but only because he hit Sam first."

Dad pulls out a chair for me and sits opposite. "What do you mean?"

"Bobby came out of nowhere and punched Sam in the nose. Sam dropped and when I tried to help him, Bobby called Sam's dad a diaper-head."

Dad's eyes grow wide. "Is Sam okay?

"I have no idea. He ran home and Mrs. Madina won't let me see him." I take a breath. "Bobby called Sam 'Osama.' Can you believe that?"

Dad nods. "Sadly, I can. It's because Sam is Muslim, and Bobby is probably lashing out at him and his family for the attacks."

"But, Sam isn't Muslim. He's American!"

"Sam is a Muslim-American or American-Muslim; I'm not sure the right way to say it. But either way, his family is Muslim."

"His grandparents are, but the rest of them aren't."

"But that's his background. He can't just change it."

I stand. "It's not like he's religious or anything—he never goes to church. He's not really a Muslim."

"You mean a mosque, not a church. And he can be Muslim without practicing Islam. It's pretty common here, and his dad once told me it's one of the reasons he moved to the states, to get away from some of the strict Islamic rules. But still, they're Muslim."

Maybe it's true, but Sam—or his family—would never hijack a plane.

Dad sighs. "Look, I have to take you to school and hope that Bobby's family will let this drop."

My head is throbbing even more. I keep the ice pack in place. "Fine, but they better call Bobby in, too. He's the one who started it all."

....

I didn't notice it this morning, but the flag in front of the school is flying at half-staff. The cars in the parking lot are covered with window flags blowing in the wind. They remind me of the military graveyards in my and Sam's magazines.

The secretary in the front office makes Dad give her his license. She scribbles his information on a clipboard and hands it to him. "Sorry. We've tightened security since Tuesday."

Dad signs the paper. "Don't be sorry. That's a good thing."

Maybe, but it won't keep people like Bobby out. We'll have to fix them ourselves.

In the hall, Officer Roth tells me to have a seat in his office. Mr. Brinkmann's sitting alone in a conference room next door.

Officer Roth motions for Dad to have a seat in a chair by the sign-in desk. "I'd like to try to handle it with just the boys first."

Dad nods in agreement.

Bobby's sitting in Officer Roth's office with a nice shiner glowing around his swollen eye. Coach Rehart's there, too, but I have no clue why.

Officer Roth closes the door and sits behind his desk. "So, what's the problem, boys?"

Bobby snaps to attention. "He jumped me!"

Coach Rehart says, "That's not what I heard." He looks at Officer Roth. "My witnesses said Bobby had Jake pinned and threw several punches before Jake managed to get him off."

His witnesses obviously didn't see the whole thing.

Bobby yells, "Jake jumped me first!"

I can get out of this. Coach will take my word for it if I deny hitting Bobby first. My rep's way better than his.

Officer Roth looks at me. "Jake?"

If I deny it, I'll avoid suspension, but . . . this is for Sam. "I did. I jumped him first," I say.

Coach Rehart's face sags. "Jake."

I don't know what he wants me to say. I can't say I'm sorry because I'm not, so I just shrug, which hurts my bruised chest.

Principal Ogden comes in and says, "Which one of you wants to tell me what happened?"

I don't hesitate. "Bobby punched Sam this morning because he thinks Sam's a terrorist."

Mr. Ogden's eyes narrow at Bobby. "Really?"

Bobby, white-knuckled, grips the chair. "That's not true. It was an accident. He ran into my elbow. Besides, it was at the park, not at school."

"He's lying!" I holler.

Officer Roth looks at me. "You're saying that Bobby beat up Sam on campus?"

"No," I say, "none of it was *on* campus. It was at the park right behind school."

"Seems that detail was left out. I'm afraid that changes things." Officer Roth leans back in his chair and rocks a few times. He gives Bobby a once-over with his eyes. Finally, he says, "If Sam's or Bobby's parents would like to file a report with the Coral Springs police, the incident will be investigated. But if it didn't happen on school property, unfortunately I can't do anything about it."

"What?" I yell. "That's not fair! Are you listening to me? Bobby threw Sam on the ground. He was bleeding. Bobby wouldn't even let me take Sam to the nurse's office."

Mr. Ogden glares at Bobby, but says to me, "Is Sam okay?"

"I don't know. I haven't seen him. What if he's not?" I lunge for Bobby. "It's all your fault!"

Coach Rehart grabs me. "Be careful, Jake. What you did was out of line, same as Bobby."

"No, it wasn't." Spit flies out of my mouth as I protest. "I was defending Sam. Bobby threw punches out of nowhere."

Mr. Ogden holds up his palm. "Bobby, go wait outside." He motions Dad in.

Bobby smirks as he passes me.

Mr. Ogden continues, "Jake, you can't just beat people up when you think they're wrong."

"I know that. But Bobby actually hit Sam. What was I supposed to do, walk away? Come tattle? What would *you* have done?"

Coach Rehart and Officer Roth both look away. They'd probably do the same thing I did but just can't say it.

Mr. Ogden sighs in Dad's direction. "Hopefully the Brinkmanns won't press charges, but keep us posted. We'll give the Madinas a call to let them know what happened and to check on Sam. You may as well take Jake home for today."

Dad nods. Before I leave, Coach and Officer Roth both shake my hand but say nothing—which kind of says a lot.

....

On the way home, Dad shouts, "I've warned you about this Brinkmann kid before! What were you thinking?"

"I was sticking up for my friend."

He grips the steering wheel. "You don't get it, do you? The Brinkmanns are not reasonable people. They're bound to press charges against you."

"Then Sam will press charges against Bobby."

He breathes heavy. "You have an answer for everything, don't you?"

"I wish I did, because then this might all make sense. How did everything get so screwed up?"

He stares at me and half laughs. "When did you get so wise?" He pulls in the driveway. "Look, when these kinds of things happen, you find out who people really are and what they stand for. Stay away from Bobby from now on, okay?"

He's right. Today I saw who Bobby really is. I think I always knew.

....

Tap, tap. I bolt upright in bed, dropping Grandpa's medal that had been clenched in my fist. *Tap, tap, tap, tap, tap.* It's Sam. I flip the locks and shove the window open.

"Hey." I stick my hand through the opening. The dark rain clouds make it seem a lot later than it is. "Something wrong with the front door?"

He grips my wrist and hauls himself over the sill, sending instant pain through my bruised chest and splattering mud onto my floor. His eyes bug out, but he doesn't answer. His nose is still swollen from this morning—like purple, black, and blue tie-dye across the middle of his face.

I close the window. "What's going on?"

He heads for my closet. "I need to borrow some stuff."

I pick up the medal and put it on my dresser. "What for?"

Sam flips through my shirts. "I just need to." He stands on his tip-toes to see my top shelf, then bends to check out the shoes.

"Is something wrong?"

Silence.

"Sam!"

He doesn't look at me. Instead, he spills the details to the Eagle's football team plastered on my wall. "My dad . . . the FBI came to my house. They think he knew them. And my mom . . ."

"You're not making any sense. The FBI's at your house?"

"Not anymore. Like I told you, my dad recognized Atta from the bank and called in a tip to the FBI hotline yesterday. He never heard back. When they showed up today, he figured that's what it was about, but the agents said they found my dad's business card with some crazy writing on the back in Atta's apartment. So they went to my dad's bank to check the video cameras. Atta was captured on video getting a ton of money from a wire transfer. My dad helped him with the transaction."

I fall back onto my bed. "But your dad didn't do anything, right? I mean, he didn't know the guy, did he?"

"Of course he didn't know him! He was just doing his job. He hands his card out to everyone who comes in."

"Yeah, but your dad called the FBI. He wouldn't do that if he had been helping Atta. That doesn't make any sense."

"I know. But what if they don't believe him? What if . . ." he trails off as he opens and closes my drawers. "Nevermind. I have a plan."

"Are they gonna come back?"

"I don't know. But my parents are fighting. Mom wants to pack up and leave. Dad told her we didn't do anything wrong so we're staying." Sam picks up his old GI Joe guy on my shelf and I remember when he and I first traded them. We agreed it didn't matter that we had the other's favorite because we'd be "friends till Martians invade the earth."

"Can I ask you a question?" I finally say.

He keeps fumbling through my stuff and doesn't answer.

"You think Bobby jumped you because you look like those terrorists?"

He's got my Philadelphia the City of Brotherly Love T-shirt in his hand and doesn't miss a beat when he replies, "Maybe. Or maybe it's my name. Who knows?"

"But you don't even believe in that Muslim stuff."

"I don't. I mean, I've only been to a mosque twice and that was because my grandfather took me to the one down the street from school when I was little. I can't change where I come from, though." He grabs a red, white, and blue bandana from the top of my dresser. "When Aamber and I were born, my dad's parents begged my mom and dad to have a baby naming ceremony for us. Names mean everything to Muslims. My parents agreed, but swore it was the only custom they'd allow until we were old enough to go to the mosque ourselves—if we ever wanted to. My dad stopped going as soon as he moved out of his parents' house."

"Why?"

"He said it just wasn't for him, and when he met my mom in college, she didn't follow the customs either."

I swivel around. "So, what's your name mean?"

"Sameed means 'brave.' I have like six other names, too. They all stand for something. My full name is Muhammad Sameed Adil Harun Yusuf Madina." He's still scouring my room for things and pacing back and forth. "But my birth certificate doesn't say that or anything. Just Sameed Madina. "

I never thought about it before, but I wonder if Jake means anything special.

"Like I said, it's the only tradition my parents have followed with Aamber and me."

Bobby must've known about Sam's name, though. "If you don't practice that religion, why would Bobby attack you?"

He stops pacing and stares me dead in the eyes. "Why would he do it even if I did?"

It's a good question. I have no answer.

He goes on, "I don't know much about Islam, so I can't even defend it, but that terrorist was nothing like my grandparents, and they're as holy as you can get. They'd never do that in the name of anyone."

I picture Bobby's face as he threw insults at Sam and me. I picture the FBI questioning Mr. Madina. It's not right. Muslim or not, Sam's parents aren't terrorists. I've known them forever and they're the nicest people in the world.

Sam sighs and flops onto my bed, holding Grandpa's medal in his hand.

I jump from my chair. "You're not taking that."

He's all serious looking. "I wouldn't borrow it if weren't important. I gotta do this."

"For real?"

He nods.

I know Sam would do the same for me if I needed something. "Fine. Take it."

"Thanks."

I hand him an old backpack to put the stuff in. "What do you think your dad's gonna do?"

"Nothing. But I'm not so sure about my mom. She's talking about going to Saudi Arabia with my dad's parents."

"My mom's been weird about this whole thing, too. What is with them?"

"You mean what happened to me?"

"No . . ." I walk over to the Eagle's team picture. "Not you. Just weird about the attacks. Maybe she thinks there'll be more or something."

"I wonder that, too. Don't you?"

"I did on Tuesday, but not now. I'm sure the fighter pilots are in their planes—locked and loaded, just waiting for a 'go.'" I look at the clock. "Do your parents know you're here?"

"No, they think I'm sleeping." He sits on my bed, taking extra long with wrapping the medal safely between the bandana and the shirt. "I'm telling you, I've never seen them scream at each other like that. I should probably get back before they flip."

"I'll see you at school tomorrow, right?"

He nods.

"Good, because Bobby might go after me again."

Sam backs away and looks at me. "You? What for?"

"I punched him after he hit you."

"Seriously?" He pats my back and I wince. "You okay?"

"Yeah, but Bobby's got a nice black eye."

Sam sticks out his fist and I bump it.

He grabs the Eagles hat from my head. "I need to borrow this, too."

"Fine. I'll walk you out. Go through the front door this time."

The rain's taking a break as we walk outside and not one, but two, cars pull into my driveway.

....

Mr. Madina stands on the stone pathway, arms clutched around Sam's chest in a bear hug. "You've made your mother sick with worry. Why didn't you ask us if you could come here?"

Sam shrugs.

Mom's behind him, arms folded over her agenda book. Dad's suddenly there, too. He must've followed me out the door.

"You're supposed to be in your room, with ice on that nose." Mr. Madina walks toward Mom and leans in to kiss her cheek as he says, "Hi."

She mumbles a hello then hurries toward the porch.

Mr. Madina says, "I'm sorry to bother you both. We didn't even know he was gone."

Dad steps off the porch, extending his hand. "No problem, Adil. I'm sorry, too. I had no idea Sam was here." Mom's lips tighten and Dad asks, "How's he feeling?"

"To be honest, I'm not sure. We got a little sidetracked this afternoon. He was asleep in his room last I checked on him."

Mom's eyebrows arch. "Sidetracked?"

"Yeah." Mr. Madina wraps his arm around Sam's shoulder. "The FBI had some questions for me. I called them yesterday to tell them that one of the terrorists had an account at my bank. I was surprised when I saw his photo on TV. He was so pleasant to me." He pauses like he's lost in a thought. "I feel guilty. If I had known, just think, maybe some of this could have been prevented."

Mom's face goes pale.

He claps Sam on the back. "Well, it's all squared away now. I didn't have much to tell them, but I hope it helps them find whatever information they need."

I hope Sam's mom will forget about leaving now that everything's all right.

Three choppers fly low and Mom flinches. The planes are slowly getting back in the air today, but the helicopters—always military looking—are still patrolling. No one's used to it.

"This whole thing is so hard to comprehend," Mr. Madina says. "My cousin works for a finance company in the second tower. He's still missing."

I cringe. I hear that the phone lines have been jammed all over New York. At least I hope that's all it is.

Mom looks at the ground and stays oddly quiet. Dad shakes his head.

Mr. Madina clears his throat. "How are you all holding up?"

I stare at Mom, waiting for her to answer, but it's Dad who finally does. "Same as everyone else, I suppose. It's a lot to take in. My brother used to work in the South tower, but was moved to a smaller office back in Philly about two months ago."

"This may sound crazy," Mr. Madina pauses, "but it's the stories like your brother's that help me get through the day. All the survivors and the close-calls are a bit of light in the midst of such horror."

Dad nods. "I hope they find your cousin."

"Thank you. We better be going," Mr. Madina says. "Kyda was a nervous wreck when we realized Sam was gone. If you all need anything, please let us know." Mr. Madina shakes Dad's hand again. Mom simply nods.

"Jake." Sam's dad sticks his hand out to me and I shake it. "We'll see you soon. Sam is lucky to have you for a friend."

....

I shuffle up the porch steps, noticing again that our house remains flagless. "Why don't we have a flag outside?"

Mom disappears through the front door ahead of me. "It's just best not to make waves," she calls back to me.

"What does that mean?"

"It means we don't need one, that's all." She takes a bottle of Excedrin from the cabinet and pops two pills into her mouth. "So much has happened today I don't even know where to begin."

Dad sets the taco fixings he prepared on the counter.

"Tell me about it," I say.

She rubs the side of her head. "I got a phone call from Mrs. Wilkey. She told me that the FBI was at the Madinas' house and she wanted to know if I knew anything. I'm surprised Adil was so open about it."

"Why wouldn't he be?" I layer taco stuff in the hard tortilla shell and head for the table. "He called them himself."

Mom makes her plate and sits. "If they're questioning him, they must not think he's totally innocent."

I mumble through a mouthful of food, "You're not serious, are you?"

She doesn't answer. I look at Dad.

He says, "I'm sure they're just doing their jobs."

Mom's voice gets louder. "I told you what Alice Wilkey said when she called. There are plenty of Muslims living here who helped these terrorists along the way. They certainly weren't acting alone."

It's a scary thought and she might be right about those guys getting help, but it definitely wasn't Sam's family, no matter what Bobby or anyone else thinks.

She pushes her plate away. "Then you"—she looks at me—"go and get yourself in a fight."

"Bobby deserved it."

Mom shakes her head. "No one deserves it."

"Well, Sam especially didn't deserve it. He didn't do anything."

"It doesn't surprise me that someone targeted him. It was bound to happen."

"What?" I yell.

"Olivia." Dad rubs her back.

"It's true," she says. "It's best if you stay away from him for now, Jake. I don't want anyone thinking you're mixed up with them."

I wipe my mouth. "You mean mixed up with the Madinas because the FBI was there? They're not the bad guys."

"How do you know?" She says it so calmly it scares me.

"Are you for real? Do you really think the Madinas are terrorists?"

"It's not that simple. Do I think they would have gotten on a plane and flown it into a building? No. But how well do we *really* know them?"

Her words choke me. Sam's practically family after all these years. "Are you serious, Mom? Mrs. Madina's your friend."

Mom doesn't look at me.

My chest is heaving. "Isn't she?"

Dad rests his hand on my arm. "Calm down. That's not what Mom means."

The Madinas are not terrorists. Mom's wrong. I want her to say that she's sorry. That she didn't mean it. "Mom?"

Nothing.

"Mom!"

My lungs feel tight—crushed. My thoughts trip over each other. It's obvious she's not going to answer. I have to get out of here. I need to run. I bolt up from the table and sprint out the garage door, slamming it behind me.

How well do we really know them? I can't believe she'd even think it. Right now, I feel like I know them better than my own family.

CHAPTER 8

September 14, 2001
Friday

....

The next morning I'm out of bed and out the door before Mom and Dad can say a word to me. I don't want an explanation; I want an apology. If they really think Sam's family could help the guys that flew planes into buildings and killed people . . . I don't know. I really don't know anything. I can't remember one time that Mom ever had a problem with the Madinas before. I sit on Sam's front porch to avoid the pelting rain and wait a full hour before he comes outside to join me.

"What's up?" He hands me today's newspaper.

I stick it in my backpack, then open an umbrella and we start walking. "My mom's acting crazy."

"Yeah, she totally backed away when my dad said hi to her yesterday. And I thought she might pass out when my dad told her about the FBI."

My face grows hot. "Sorry about that. Everything has her spooked since the attacks."

Aamber and Katie pass us at the corner, but none of us throw insults.

Sam and I walk in silence for a while, then he says, "If you want, I can just stay away for a while. I don't want to make things worse for you."

"That's stupid. Mom's just out of it right now. She'll be fine." At least I hope she will.

Sam shakes George's hand as we slosh across the nearly flooded intersection. The front of the school is packed, mostly because the side gates are still locked. A group of cops stand guard.

There's a swarm of kids laughing as Sam and I walk down the main hall. When the crowd parts, I see a diaper taped to the front of Sam's locker. Bobby waves as he turns the corner, a roll of duct tape around his wrist like one of Grandma's bracelets.

"Chicken!" I yell after him, but he's already gone.

Sam rips the diaper off his locker, and I shove it in my backpack.

"I have a plan," I say.

He smiles.

....

In Social Studies, Mrs. Cruz taped names to each of our desks. Mine and Sam's are together, along with Aamber's. Bobby is clear on the other side of the room. She must have had a heads up about our fight yesterday.

Mrs. Cruz comes in and we write down the journal question as she takes attendance. *What is the purpose of studying history?* Finally, one I can answer.

Mom's always said, *History is important so we know when to repeat it and when not to.* Even though I've heard her say it at least thirty times, she never goes into more detail. I used to ask her back when I was little, but now I know. I get it. I whip out my notebook and jot my answer.

Coach Rehart sticks his head into our room and asks to see me and Sam.

I hear Bobby say, "They're finally taking out the trash."

I want to deck him again, but I see Coach Rehart standing outside shaking his head. He closes the door behind us.

Coach puts his hand on Sam's shoulder, "Listen, boys. We need to have a meeting after school. Since it was front page news, you'll find out soon enough that the authorities are assuming Kirk's dad was one of the people killed at the Pentagon on Tuesday. He was in a meeting in the wing that got hit, and they haven't located him yet. I know you boys are friends with . . ."

I tune Coach out and lean against the wall, pressing myself hard to keep from falling over, which I'm sure I'm about to do. It's got to be a mistake. They're going to find Kirk's dad. All of a sudden, the whole world feels small—and not in a good way.

I heard Sam say, "But they're not positive he's dead, right? I mean, he might just show up and be fine."

Coach says, "Despite not having found his body, they're 99 percent sure he's gone."

Yeah, but there's still a 1-percent chance he's okay. I'm sure Kirk's holding on to that slim chance. I would.

....

All morning my thoughts shift from Kirk to Bobby and back. Kirk's not in school, but Bobby is, and Sam and I are going to make him pay for the diaper thing.

We pass a vending machine on the way to the cafeteria and I stick money in. "You pick."

Sam pushes C2 and out pops a Snickers bar.

"Good choice." I shove it in my backpack so it'll get nice and warm before school ends.

....

After school, we make a mad-dash for the bike racks. On

the way, I unwrap the Snickers and Sam holds out the diaper. I plop the candy bar in, he folds the diaper in half, smushes it around, and then opens it up to look. With the rain falling on it, it's extra gross.

"Sick," I say.

He laughs.

We smear it, chocolate side down, all over the seat of Bobby's bike and tape the diaper around it. Then we wait outside the fence for Bobby to come. He's talking up some girl as they share an umbrella, and he doesn't notice the diaper till he starts to unlock the bike.

"What the?" He looks around, then spots us. "Wow, good one, babies." When he takes the diaper off, the girl shrieks. Then she laughs—at Bobby. And so do Sam and I as the three of us walk away in the pouring rain.

Bobby yells, "You'll be sorry!"

But we won't, because the look on his face and the girl ditching him are priceless.

....

At the team meeting, Coach ushers us to the bleachers in the gym. "The county won't let us start practice again until Monday, but I wanted to call a meeting anyway."

Some kids grumble.

He holds his hands up. "Listen up. As you probably

know by now, the authorities think Kirk's dad was killed in the attack on the Pentagon. I've spoken with the family and they're doing as best they can right now."

I can't help but think if Mr. Steiner had been late to work that day. Or sick. Or if he'd come home to see Kirk race against Palmetto on Tuesday instead.

Coach goes on. "I expect there will be a funeral sometime next week. It would be nice if you all attended as a team and supported Kirk's family, though of course it's not mandatory. Kirk might be new, but he's one of us."

Everyone sits in silence, averting their gaze from one another.

Coach finishes, "The county issued us a new schedule." He passes papers around. "As you can see, we race Palmetto next week. Try to get a run or two in over the weekend." He claps once. "That's it. Go on home."

On our way out, I say to Sam. "We should try to find Kirk's house and go see him."

Sam doesn't answer.

I elbow him in the arm. "Right? I'm sure he could use some friends."

Sam picks up his pace. "I don't know. He might not want to see us right now." He heads away from me, back into the school, and yells over his shoulder, "I'm supposed to meet Aamber in the broadcasting room. I'll catch you later."

Sam is acting strange, but since Dad's waiting in the parking lot, I let it go. I don't know what I'd do if my dad was dead. And I don't know what I'll say to Kirk at the funeral, but I know I need to see him. The night Kirk slept at Sam's with me, all I could think about was how lucky he was. His dad was in the Navy. I wanted to meet Mr. Steiner and ask him all about warships. Now he's dead. Suddenly I get why Kirk just wanted to play Madden. It's his way to escape reality.

....

After dinner, Dad asks me to go for a run and—despite my bruised chest—it's exactly what I need. We jog in silence. The puddles on the pavement splatter water up my legs and the sound of sloshing almost drowns out Dad's huffing and puffing. We pass in front of The Oasis and I stop dead. Yellow *Do Not Enter* tape blocks off the bottom corner apartment. A cop car fortifies the front, blocking the news vans that are camped out in the parking lot. The entire scene makes my stomach lurch.

"Is this where that terrorist lived?" I ask Dad.

"Yeah."

The hairs on my neck prickle. Rigo lives in this complex, too. Coral Springs isn't that big, but still, I never thought Atta lived this close to me. Sam could be right—maybe we have seen Atta before.

The question that has ricocheted through my brain for the last two days spills out of my mouth. "Why do you think Atta wanted to live here in Coral Springs?"

"I don't know," Dad says. "Maybe because it's unassuming? No one would have questioned him here. It's pretty safe."

I've never been scared living here before, but everything is so different now. Nothing makes sense anymore.

Dad says, "Why don't we head home?"

Home is the last place I want to be. "We just started. You tired already?"

"Me? Pfft." Dad holds his side. "Where to?"

"I'll beat you to Mullins Park. If you lose, you have to buy me an ice cream."

Dad nods. "And if you lose?"

"Good one, Dad." I glance at the apartments one more time. I wonder if Rigo's family will move. I've run by here so many times; I can't help but think that maybe Atta had watched me and that sends a chill down my spine, despite the humid weather.

I dart north toward Mullins, not even looking back to make sure Dad's following. At the park, police lights flash in front of the gymnasium. My heart thumps. What if there *are* more terrorists? I stop to let Dad catch up.

"I forgot." Dad stretches to see over the crowd. "I heard something about a memorial service tonight."

Up ahead, I watch Officer Roth and another police man lead some guy away from the group of people who have gathered. The three men cross the street. They let go of the guy when they reach the opposite corner, just as a kid rushes to catch up to them. It's Bobby. Suddenly, I realize that the man is Mr. Brinkmann.

I'm close enough to hear the officers tell him that he can't come back to the service with the sign he's holding, so he waves it in their faces but stays where he's told. Then he spots Dad and me and gives us the middle finger. So does Bobby.

"Nice family," Dad says.

I'd flick them off right back if Dad weren't here.

Mr. Brinkmann flashes the sign at cars passing on the street. It reads: *In the name of Allah, all Muslims go to hell! Honk if you agree.*

A few cars honk. I can't believe other people actually agree with him!

Dad grabs my shoulder and guides me closer to the crowd.

Rows of police cars line the street. Two fire engines are parked in front of the entrance to the gym. Their ladders tower above the crowd, angled together and pointing toward the sky. As "The Star Spangled Banner" booms in the background, the crowd stares as one fire-fighter climbs each ladder and drapes an American flag between them. In the windy, cloud-filled sky, the flag flaps, unlike my breath, which is still.

Dad palms my shoulder. "Do you want to go home?"

I scan the crowd. Gobs of people decked out in red, white, and blue suck me in. I want to be a part of this. "Go? No, we can't leave." A warmth creeps into me and it's the best I've felt in days.

I grab Dad's arm and pull him deeper into the swarm of people. A little boy next to me tugs on my shirt. I bend. His T-shirt's scribbled with marker and reads GOD BLESS AMERICA. His arms are painted with red and blue stars. He passes me a box. I grab it with one hand and pull out two white candles for Dad and me. Like a wave going around a football stadium, people plop down on the grass, sidewalk, and benches. Dad and I sit on a parking bumper. Slowly, one candle after another begins to glow and the darkening sky fills with flickering yellow flames. I cup my candle to keep it from blowing out with the wind.

Mayor Beck turns on the podium microphone. "Thank you all for coming. Let's hope Tropical Storm Gabrielle holds off for a while so we can continue our memorial. Our hearts go out to the people who have lost their lives in the tragedy that occurred three days ago. Several of the lives lost were current and past residents of our city. You can see the memorial board over here on my left that the peer counseling class at Mangrove Middle created. Each heart represents a resident or family member of a resident of our city who has died or is still missing as a result of the attacks."

It's hard to see for sure, but it looks like there are six hearts. Six people just from our town? How is that possible? New York City and DC are like a thousand miles away.

"We'd like to send our deepest sympathies to each of them, especially the Steiner family who is with us here tonight. Max Steiner was a commander in the United States Navy and perished in the Pentagon attack. Several others were—"

I want to plug my ears. Kirk. I have to find him.

I block out the mayor's speech and kneel so I can scan the crowd. Matt's off to the side of me. I wave. He gives me a tight smile then looks away. What's up with him?

I see Mr. Madina next. He holds an umbrella over Sam's and Aamber's heads near a light pole a few parking spaces over. Mr. Madina has a small flag tucked into his shirt pocket. Sam sees me and points toward the fire truck on the right. Kirk's sitting on a folding chair with his mom and three sisters. The girls are all sobbing. Kirk's staring off into space, his hands balling and unballing the tie around his neck.

I fall back next to Dad, zoning in and out while different people speak. My brain switches back and forth from their words to the pictures I've stored or created in my head: the people in the World Trade Center, Sam on the ground, Sam's dad being grilled by the FBI, Mom's single tear in the car, and now Kirk—who's dadless.

The memorial service ends with a song I've never heard before. As it plays on, everyone begins to stand. A few people are outright sobbing. The lady next to me is moving to the music with her hand over her chest. I look at Dad and his eyes are wet. My heart squeezes. I close my eyes, hoping the drops that are stinging the corners of my eyes won't fall.

Dad's arm locks around my shoulder as the song ends. The crowd claps. Whistles fill the sticky air. When I open my eyes, my body jolts unexpectedly. I'm suddenly face to face with Bobby. My smile fades as I toe the imaginary line between us, ready for battle. Rigo's right behind him. I see Sam walking toward us.

"Don't you think that boy of yours needs to be caged up for a while?" Mr. Brinkmann spits the words into Dad's face.

Bobby smirks.

Dad keeps his arm dead-bolted on my shoulder. "Hello, Dale."

Sam moves closer, off to the side behind Rigo. I hope Mr. Brinkmann doesn't see him. If Bobby's dad starts picking on Sam in front of everyone, there's sure to be another confrontation. I glance over at Kirk's family. It doesn't seem right to fight in front of them. Not now.

"What are you teaching this boy?" Mr. Brinkmann stops short of poking his finger in my chest. "You're letting him run around with rag-heads?"

I swat his finger away and brace myself. Dad steps in front of me—he'd never let Mr. Brinkmann treat me like that. I move to the side, ready to pounce on Bobby when Dad takes a swing at Mr. Brinkmann.

"I'm sorry about the incident yesterday." Dad looks at Bobby. "Are you okay?"

My face twists as I jerk to look at Dad. He can't be serious!

Despite his black eye, Bobby laughs. "Of course, I'm okay."

"Jake's sorry, too." Dad nudges me. "Right?"

"Heck no. I'm not sorry at all."

Dad grabs me by the shoulder and jams his thumb into my skin. "Shake his hand, Jake. Tell him you're sorry and let it drop."

I look into Dad's eyes, which are narrowed at me.

He's off his chain. I don't move and he grips me tighter. It actually hurts.

I stick out my hand, but refuse to look at Bobby, and mumble, "Sorry."

Bobby shakes it and says, "Thank you. Next time, I won't go easy on you."

Mr. Brinkmann snickers.

I clench Bobby's hand harder than a world champion arm wrestler. He flinches a little before he pulls his arm back, then spits on the ground, barely missing my feet.

I take a step forward, but Dad pushes me back.

"Come on, Jake." He balls a chunk of my shirt in his fist and yanks me away. "Let's go."

"But—" I try to dig my feet into the cement. It's too wet, though, and his grip is too tight.

"*Now!*" he says through gritted teeth.

I jerk my head back and give Bobby my best evil-eyed stare. This isn't over.

Sam's already walking away and doesn't even look back at me. I'm glad he moved before the Brinkmanns saw him.

Dad releases me from his clutch once we reach the corner. He jogs across the intersection. "That man gets my veins raging!"

I hang back and keep pace several feet behind him.

If Grandpa had been there tonight, instead of dad, he would have defended me. He was a real soldier and not afraid of anything—especially not Mr. Brinkmann.

As we turn into our neighborhood, Dad flips around to face me, still jogging. "Guess I owe you an ice cream, huh?"

I speed past him without a second glance.

He catches up to me as we reach our driveway. "No ice cream, then?"

I plop down on the porch step and unlace my wet sneakers. It's one thing for Bobby to turn on Sam, but for my own dad to turn on me?

"Jake." Dad parks himself directly in front of me. "Are you ignoring me?"

Grabbing my shoes, I stand and head for the front door.

"What's the matter?"

I swing around. "How could you?" I shake my head. "How could you apologize to them for me?"

"What you did was wrong. I understand why you hit Bobby, but it doesn't make it okay."

"Are you kidding me? What about what he did to Sam?"

"That's not my issue. Or yours. You can't change the mind of a bigot. And throwing punches doesn't solve anything."

"So, you're just supposed to let them get away with it?"

"What did you want me to do, hit Mr. Brinkmann? Yell and scream and cause a scene?"

"Yes!" I holler. "But instead, you're just all I'm-so-sorry-my-son's-a-jerk. It was pathetic." My energy drains suddenly. "You're afraid of them, aren't you?"

Dad's eyes widen. "Is that what you think?"

I nod.

"This has nothing to do with fear." He wipes his fore-head with the sleeve of his shirt. "How can you stand up to someone who's not capable of reasoning?"

I shake my head as I look at him. "How can you not?"

....

Dad kept trying to explain himself after our argument but not a word of it made sense to me. Eventually, I gave up and went to my room.

I grab the newspaper from my desk and flip through it. Mr. Steiner looks just like Kirk staring up from the front page. On the next page, there's an article about Atta. They found a *Qur'an* in his car at the airport. It mentions Allah and words I can't even pronounce. My brain's on overload. I need to sleep, but can't. There are too many thoughts. I need something to get my mind off things. Something that has nothing to do with all the craziness of the last few days.

I creep down to the living room and flip through the TV stations until I reach ESPN. "In case you're just joining us, the NFL has decided to postpone this weekend's games until January sixth and seventh in an effort to support the families of the terrorist attacks."

Stop. Just stop. No more! I flip the channel again to the old standby station and watch reruns of *The Cosby Show*. Something normal. My eyes grow heavy, and I shove a pillow under my head as I watch the Huxtable family sing for their grandparents' anniversary.

CHAPTER 9

SEPTEMBER 15, 2001
SATURDAY

....

My chest is still sore, but the lump on the back of my head's almost gone. I carefully slip on a red Phillies T-shirt and drag myself to the kitchen for a granola bar. Mom and Dad are MIA.

There's no sun at all, and the ground is soaked so I can't cut the Wilkeys' grass, but Mom left me a note that I still have to go over and see if they need anything, which stinks. I head to Sam's first, hoping he'll help me.

In front of Sam's house, Mr. Madina shakes hands with a guy in a suit through the window of a big black SUV.

Sam comes from the garage wearing my Eagles hat and his way-too-small D.A.R.E. shirt from fifth grade that has a big American flag on it. His nose looks even worse today. He sticks mini flags all over his yard—the ones we used on Halloween a few years ago when he and I dressed up as American soldiers. We left them on territories we conquered and, in one afternoon, our entire street looked like someone had confused Halloween with the Fourth of July. At least the Madinas are showing their American pride. I don't get why Mom won't let us hang a flag on our house.

I cross the grass toward Sam as the SUV pulls away. I see a government license plate on the car.

"Who was that?"

"It's no big deal." Sam stabs another flag into the ground.

"Was it the FBI again?"

"Yeah, but so what? They just had a few more questions about Atta for my dad."

"Like what?"

"Why are you bothering me about this? You're worse than a mom."

That's as bad as saying I run like a girl.

He moves to another section of the yard. I don't follow, keeping some distance between us.

Maybe he feels bad because he looks at me and explains, "They wanted to know if Atta mentioned any names or anything when my dad was with him. And if he spoke English. Stuff like that. See, no big deal."

If they're fishing for more names, they definitely think there might be more terrorists in the country—maybe even in Coral Springs.

"Did your dad know anything?"

"No!" Sam snaps. "He already told them everything he remembers."

"Okay, geez." I reach for some of the flags in his hand. "Want me to help? I have to go to the Wilkeys in a little while and work. Want to come?"

He pulls his arm back. "Can't. I'm busy today."

Mr. Madina comes over and shakes my hand. "Hi, Jake. What's up?"

I shrug. "Nothing. Just seeing if Sam wants to help me next door."

Mr. Madina nods. "Of course, he'll help. You better hurry, though. The rain's about to start up again. Let's hope this storm doesn't stall right over us. We've had enough rain to last months."

"But Dad . . ."

So Sam's not really busy after all. But what's he so mad about?

"Go on, Sam." Mr. Madina motions toward the street corner. "Your friend needs help."

Sam drops the flags on the grass and shuffles over to the Wilkeys' with me.

"What's wrong with you?" I finally ask.

"Whatever. Let's just get this over with so I can go home."

I grab his arm to stop him. "What is up with you?"

He yanks free of me. "You. You're up. And your mom. I tried to let it go when your mom was all weird to me and my dad the other day. But then . . . then you go and shake hands with Bobby last night. For real? I should ask *you* what's up."

"Well, go ahead and ask. I never wanted to shake Bobby's hand. My dad made me. Do you think I'd shake it on purpose? I wanted to punch his face in."

Sam stands silently.

I pull my shirt up and show him my bruised chest. "Are you forgetting that I hit him for you? I can't *stand* him."

He still says nothing.

"I told you yesterday that my mom's freaking out. She's just scared, but she'll come around."

His head droops. "I know." He takes a seat on the Wilkeys' porch steps. "I'm sorry."

I sit next to him. "Forget about it. Nothing's been right these last few days."

"You have no idea."

"What do you mean?"

He looks toward his house and waits a few seconds before saying, "I guess I'm just sick of people assuming

I'm a whacko or a terrorist. Muslims aren't bad. At least not from what I've been reading."

"What are you reading?"

He swishes water off the porch step between us with his hand. "I've been reading about Islam and Muslims. If Bobby's going to accuse me of being one, I might as well know more about them. I should have paid more attention when my grandfather used to tell me stuff about it."

"Who cares what Bobby says?"

"It's not about Bobby, but I'm glad I looked all that stuff up. My grandparents are the most peaceful people I know, and they'd never be in a religion that wants to kill people. But I wanted to see what Islam was for myself."

"Well, if Islam is peaceful, why'd those guys fly planes into innocent people?"

"They didn't!" Sam practically yells at me and I jump. Then, more calmly he says, "I mean, those terrorists were just crazy guys that hated the US. Even the Islamic leaders say the hijackers weren't true Muslims."

I read that in the paper, but who knows what to believe any more. If it's true, it's good defense for us against Bobby, his dad, and all those other jerks who were honking their horns last night. Still, it's a little strange that Sam's so interested in Islam all of a sudden. And that he's getting mad so easily.

The rain picks up and I look to the front door. There's

a rake and a note attached to it. I scale the steps in one hop. *Please clean the leaves from the storm drain grate at the end of the driveway. That's all for today. The rake can go back in the shed when you're done.* I'm about to turn back around when I notice the window next to the door is cracked open, but all the others are shut tight. It's freaky.

"Looks like a one man operation. I got this," I tell Sam.

He stands. "You sure?"

"Yeah. Hey, I have to go to my grandma's later, but maybe we can run if it ever stops raining?"

"We might have to run to catch a ride on Noah's ark if it doesn't."

I crack up. Sam's the best.

....

When I come back from putting the rake in the shed, the front window's sealed and there's a green Gatorade along with a sticky note attached to a newspaper on the top step. I reach for the paper and the note: *Thank you.* No signature. There's a twenty-dollar bill inside. Mom never mentioned I'd get paid and I don't feel right taking their money so I leave it on the porch table next to the front door. I grab the Gatorade, shove the paper under my shirt, and head home in the rain.

As I jog, I think about Sam checking out the Muslim stuff. I don't know why it's sticking with me, but it is.

....

The ride to Grandma's is silent. I've barely talked to Mom since Thursday when she told me to stay away from Sam. While she and Grandma clean up the lunch dishes, I head to Grandpa's den. It hasn't changed at all since I was a kid. I pick up a picture of Grandpa in a suit. He's standing in front of a big building with gates all around it and the street signs are written in another language. I've seen it at least thirty times, but it's the first time I wonder why he's not in his military uniform. I set the frame down. Next to the picture is a paper folded like a bird. It used to be dark blue, but I swear every time I come it's more faded. I wish I could talk to Grandpa and ask him what kind of missions he went on. I wish I knew who killed him. He'll always be a hero, but it would be better if I knew his whole story.

Grandma glides—her version of walking—into the room. "That," she points to the crane in my hand, "was one of your grandpa's most prized possessions."

"Really? Did Mom make it for him?" I ask. Since Mom never talks about Grandpa, I hope to get some real stories from Grandma.

"No. Some little girl in the Middle East gave it to him when he was overseas."

"Seriously?" I flip it over, inspecting the creases.

"Yep, it's a symbol of peace, you know? You wanna play cards?" She flops Indian-style on the couch and tucks her flowy white skirt under her legs.

I put the crane back on the shelf and sit.

She says, "Go Fish?"

"War."

Her bracelets jingle as she deals. A few cards in, I'm already losing as I spill the story about Sam and Bobby, and what Mom said about the Madinas. Grandma nods the whole time. She's good like that. She just listens and doesn't lecture me.

When I'm done she says, "You need to keep trusting your gut. That's what it's there for."

"What do you think Grandpa would do if he were me?"

"Oh, I know what he'd do. He was a good judge of character. So are you."

I smile.

"And since you asked . . ." She throws a card. "He'd also give your mom a break."

Grandma keeps saying I'm just like Grandpa, but maybe I'm not. Not if he'd forgive Mom without getting her to change her mind.

Grandma pats my leg. "I'm not saying she's right. I'm just saying she needs some time to adjust with everything that's happened this week. So, will you give her that?"

"Sam's my best friend, though. I'm not going to stop hanging out with him just because Mom's suddenly afraid that his family is helping terrorists."

"No, and I don't expect you to. Look at me." She sets her cards down, cups my chin in her hands, and says right into my eyes, "I promise you, your mom doesn't believe that."

I want to believe Grandma. I *really* do. But I'm not sure I can.

"After your grandpa died, she was angry and blamed a lot of people. She was in a bad place for a long time. Over the years, every time a bomb's gone off or we were attacked in some way, your mom's gone right back to that bad place. This time, well, it's so close to home and so many innocent people were hurt . . . she's scared. She doesn't trust too many people."

I'm trying hard to get what Mom must be feeling. She was my age when her dad died, and a few days ago I thought my own dad might be missing. Then there's Kirk, whose dad *is* dead. It all stinks, but I still don't get how any of this could make Mom think the Madinas would help out some terrorists.

Grandma plays a card. "Your mom is going to be fine. Trust me, okay?"

I nod and flip a card.

She takes both of them. "All you have to do is keep your mom in mind before you say things. For now, she doesn't need to hear you talk about Sam and his family."

I nod again and agree to give Mom a break. For now.

I clear my throat. "Do you think we'll go to war because of this? I mean, someone's got to pay for the attacks, right?"

"Oh, honey." She smoothes out her skirt. "It's a crazy time we're living in, huh?" She pauses. "I have a feeling we will go to war, but honestly I hope we don't. I don't think it's the answer."

I'm completely shocked. Grandpa died protecting our country, and I thought for sure Grandma would agree that we need to retaliate—show the bad guys who's boss. The confusion must show on my face.

"Don't give me that look, Jake. War is not always the answer, and I honestly don't know what it would solve to attack anyone right now."

She sounds like Aamber and nothing like Grandpa.

She adds, "Just a drop of water."

How can she say that, like it was nothing? Attacking

our country is a big deal. My head's too full to argue with her so I flip over my last card—a four.

She plays a nine and beats me, like always.

....

The rain is pounding down again as we head home. I wish the storm would hurry up and pass. Mom's been quiet the whole ride. I hope Grandma's right—that Mom didn't mean what she said about the Madinas. I have to try to make everything normal again so Mom will snap out of it.

I close the car door. "Want to watch a movie tonight? You can pick."

Mom puts her arm around my shoulder and opens the door from the garage to the kitchen. "Yeah. That sounds great. How about *Stuart Little*?"

There's something creepy about that mouse, but it's Mom's favorite movie. "Okay. I'll make popcorn."

Dad helps me in the kitchen while Mom looks for the movie. I grab a bowl from the cabinet.

"I can't stop thinking about things, Dad. Like, what if Mr. Steiner had come home early to see Kirk run that day? Then he'd still be here. Or what if Atta never used Mr. Madina's bank? Then the FBI wouldn't have questioned them and Mom would be okay with Sam. Or what if someone had found out about that stupid plan to attack us and we stopped it? That whole day would never have happened. It makes my head want to burst."

Dad touches my shoulder. "Believe me, I think about all that, too. I'm sure everyone in America does. But the 'what ifs' will haunt you if you let them. Just remember, you can't change what happened, so find a way to deal with it as best you can."

I'm trying my best to deal with it, but the problem is, I don't know how to get the voices in my head to shut off. Dad's right. They haunt me.

CHAPTER 10

....

I barely slept, and my eyes are heavy as I sit next to Dad in church. For the first time that I know of, Mom skips Mass. I fumble through the motions: sit, stand, bless myself, sit again.

Father O'Reilley stands for the homily, and I try not to doze off as I slouch in my seat. He talks about the terrorist attacks and about Atta living in our community.

I swear he's looking at me when he says, "We cannot let fear control us. We must live as brothers and sisters, differences and all. God has given us the power of free will—"

He mumbles on, but I'm stuck on the words *free will*. The terrorists had free will to fly planes into our buildings. And Bobby had free will to beat up Sam. It doesn't seem fair.

"—it's okay to be angry." Father O'Reilly balls his fist and shakes it in front of his chest. "It's part of our grieving process. After all, how can one make sense of such a tragedy?"

Angry is exactly what I am.

"But, it's most important that you not let the anger take over. We must channel our fear and anger and do something positive instead. Imagine if the firefighters, police officers, and countless other volunteers had let their anger and fear control them in the minutes and days following the attacks. There would have been no rescue missions. Those survivors pulled from the rubble would not be alive. So, while it's okay to be angry and afraid, those emotions must eventually be replaced with hope."

It's good knowing someone thinks it's okay to be angry. Because I'm *angry*. At Bobby for hitting Sam. At the terrorists who flew the planes and the others who planned it. At Mom for shunning the Madinas. At Dad for making me shake hands with Bobby. At Sam for acting weird. At the school for canceling our meet against Palmetto. And, truthfully, it doesn't seem like the anger will go away any time soon.

....

After dinner, as I'm finishing up my current events home-work, Dad walks into my room and sits on my bed.

"Listen, champ. I have to leave again tomorrow."

I swivel in my desk chair to face him. "What?"

"I wish I didn't. I tried to postpone it at least one more week, but they'll fire me if I don't go."

"You can't get on a plane." The blood under my skin is hot. My heart picks up pace like it's running its own cross country meet.

"I'm going to have to fly eventually; it's part of my job. You know that. We can't stop living our lives just because of what happened. Will it be safe tomorrow? Next week? A month from now? Who knows, but we have to try to get back to normal."

I want things to go back to the way they're supposed to be, but not if it means Dad has to fly. "What if there's another hijacker on your plane, though?"

"Everyone on that plane is going to be on high alert. No one's going to try anything."

"But . . ." I have to find a reason to make him stay. I can't let him leave. "What about Mom? She's acting weird. You can't leave me with her."

"Yeah, she's a little edgy, but Grandma said she'd come and stay here if either of you need her to."

I get up and scowl at my Eagles poster. If they'd played today, we could have made cheesesteaks and watched the game together—something normal. But even the NFL is messed up from the attacks. "I don't get why your job is more important than your family."

He stands. "That's not fair. It's not like I want to go, but what choice do I have? We have bills to pay."

"So, find a new job. Why do you always have to travel anyway?" I don't know why I'm trying to make Dad feel like dirt. I know he'd stay if he could, but none of this is fair. Not for him. Not for me. Not for anyone.

Dad's mouth makes a perfect O, though nothing comes out. He looks like I punched him in the gut. He sits again and seems lost in his head. I pushed him too far. Stupid. Stupid.

I sit next to him. "I'm sorry. I know you have to go. I'll take care of Mom."

He nods. "You know, I never knew your grandfather, and yet all I ever hear is that you're just like him. Only just now you were like your mom. Exactly. So maybe she's just like her dad too. Maybe you're all the same."

I have no clue what he's talking about and, for a second, I think he's lost his mind, but then he gives me a hug. "I'll be in Atlanta this week. The hotel number's on the fridge. Love you. Now get some rest."

I'm confused by him saying I'm like Mom. That's a

first, and I'm not sure I like it, especially now, because she's so scared of everything and I'm not. I reach for Grandpa's medal before I remember that Sam has it. I really need to get it back.

CHAPTER 11
SEPTEMBER 17, 2001
MONDAY

....

Mom's crying wakes me, and I rush to her bedroom. Her face is buried in the pillow but it doesn't drown out her sobs. Dad's side of the bed is empty and his suitcase, which is always packed next to his dresser on Sunday night, is gone.

I sit on the bed next to her. I'm not sure if I should hug her or leave her alone. "You okay?" I finally ask.

She grabs me around my shoulders, then pulls me down, smothering me in one long hug. I'll feel better once she stops crying. Once Dad's home again. Once everything goes back to the way it's supposed to be.

After a few seconds, I pull myself up and sit. I'm pretty sure she's crying because Dad's gone, but I decide to ask anyway. "Are you sad because Dad left?"

Snot drips from her nose. "Security at the airport is going to be a lot longer now. He had to get there extra early and didn't want to wake you."

It was hard enough to say goodbye to him last night. I'm glad he didn't wake me this morning to do it all over again. I go to the bathroom and grab a box of tissues. "Here. Want me to make you breakfast?" It's clear she won't be cooking.

"No, I'm not hungry. But grab something for yourself, okay?" She blows her nose. "I'm already going to be late today."

....

Sam and I jog to school—sort of a mini-practice. The sun's finally back and it's sticky out.

"I guess we can't count on Bobby to help us get back at Tyler during the Palmetto meet now," I say. "I'll just have to do it myself."

We cross the intersection and Sam shakes George's hand, then he says, "You can't be serious."

"What do you mean?"

"About Tyler. You're not still going through with the plan, are you?"

"Why wouldn't we?"

We stop near the entrance to the school. Sam takes a small towel out of his backpack and wipes sweat from his face. "I don't know. It just doesn't seem to matter anymore."

My eyes bug out. "You're joking, right?"

He doesn't answer.

"Right?"

"It won't fix anything. It's not going to make Tyler suddenly be nice to you." Sam turns abruptly and heads toward Cruz's class.

I stand there, floored. Tyler's a punk. I won't let him get away with embarrassing me last year. He's going to see how it feels, even if I have to get my revenge all alone.

....

Things have been strange with Sam all day—for the first time ever, it's hard to find stuff to talk about—but I still go and sit with him at lunch. Aamber, Katie, and Ian are there, too. Matt used to sit with us, but now he's a few tables over, sitting with his basketball team.

I set my tray down and take a seat at the end near Aamber, just as Bobby and Rigo walk by.

Bobby reaches over both Sam and Aamber and swipes the hamburgers off their plates. He turns to his audience of cafeteria kids and says loudly, "Look at this. The towel heads are eating meat."

A few kids laugh. Sam's face is brighter than a lit bomb. Aamber clenches my arm.

Bobby gets in Sam's face. "We all know it's against your religion to eat animals. You can't feast on one of your own, you pigs." He spits on their burgers.

Sam and I jump off the bench at the same time. I lunge for Bobby, but Sam holds me back and says to him, "Get your facts straight so you don't look dumb next time. Nothing you're saying is true."

I want to punch the smoke out of Bobby. Why is Sam holding me back?

One of the cafeteria monitors comes over. "Everything okay here?"

Before I can speak, Sam says, "It's fine." Then he sits. He totally let Bobby get away with it.

The lady points at us. "Good. Now the rest of you take your seats."

I do, but can't understand Sam at all. Once the monitor lady is gone, I stick out my foot and trip Bobby as he walks away. He stumbles and falls directly into a trash can, landing face first in a heap of smelly, lumpy food that sprawls across the floor. The entire cafeteria cracks up—at least it seems like everyone. But not Sam.

....

Sam and I change in the locker room after school for practice. I grab one of my sneakers from the bag. "You okay?"

"Yeah, why?"

"You just seem . . ."

"I'm fine." He slips his running shirt over his head.

"What about this morning? And at lunch you totally let Bobby get away with what he did."

"What could I do? I'm not going to fight him and get in trouble. He's not worth it. Besides, I can't fix his stupidity."

We head out toward the back of the school.

I stretch my legs. "But what about Tyler? What about our plan?"

"I don't know. I'm sorry. It's just not that big of a deal anymore. So many other things have happened and Tyler isn't important."

"How can you say that? You know how he embarrassed me."

"So, beat him. Beat him fair and square. That'll embarrass him enough." Sam squats and comes back up. As he squats again, he says, "You guys are going to be teammates in high school, so you should let it go."

I planned to beat him fairly. Throwing water on him was just a bonus.

Coach calls us over and we sit on the grass to finish stretching. He says, "It's been confirmed that the funeral for Mr. Steiner is tomorrow. I hope to see all of you there. It'll mean something to Kirk."

I suddenly realize that I forgot to ask Mom and Dad about attending the funeral, but I plan to be there. No matter what.

"We'll talk more about it after practice." Coach gives us the signal to go and as soon as he's out of sight, I run toward the street instead of the woods.

Sam hollers, "Where you going?"

"I'm going to run the pavement today. I need to check on my mom. She was pretty messed up about my dad leaving. Catch you later." I'm glad to run alone. Sam's acting way too strange and I don't have anything to say to him.

I take a right out of the school and hear footsteps on the cement behind me.

Sam bangs into me as he runs by. "We won't beat Palmetto like this, but I'll go with you."

We've had more disagreements these last few days

than in the whole time I've known him, but this—him running with me to check on Mom—is why we're friends. I shoulder bump him back and we run.

....

When we get to City Hall, he says, "If your mom's upset, maybe I should wait outside."

Yeah, it's best if he waits outside. I don't need Mom to see us together.

Mom's desk is front and center of Representative Hugh M. Baldwin's office. When I walk in, Uncle Hugh pulls me to his chest and noogies my head.

"Just because you turned thirteen doesn't mean I'm giving you permission to keep growing." He lets go and stands back to look at me. "Olivia, what are you feeding this boy? I swear he's shot up a foot in just a few weeks."

I haven't noticed, but I hope he's right. Longer legs will definitely help my cross country times. Mom smiles. She looks okay, and I feel better.

He leads me to some chairs off to the side of the room. "Come, sit. What are you doing here?"

"I'm at cross country practice but skipped the woods today to come say hi." I look at Mom. "Tomorrow is Mr. Steiner's funeral. Coach asked the whole team to go. Can you take me?"

She hands me a bottled water. "No, I'm sorry, but you don't need to go."

"But my whole team's going!"

Uncle Hugh stands, heads over to Mom, and puts his hand on her shoulder. "You know, I'm going to the funeral, Olivia. I don't mind taking him with me. It's okay if you can't make it."

Mom inhales deeply then turns to me. "Why do you have to do this? I don't want you to go."

I blurt, "It's not about you. It's about Kirk."

She scoffs.

Uncle Hugh raises his voice. "Jake, you know not to talk to your mom like that. This isn't an ordinary situation. Why don't you go finish your run and let me talk with her?"

I grab my water bottle, shove the door open, and run.

Sam hops off the bench and tries to keep up with me but my feet are flying.

I pump my arms hard. "She's so annoying."

"Hold up." He catches me, grabs my arm, and pulls us to a stop. "What happened?"

"She's telling me I can't go to the funeral tomorrow," I pant. "Can you believe it? Just because she doesn't want to go, doesn't mean she shouldn't let me. Right?"

He doesn't answer.

I pace. "I haven't even had a chance to see Kirk—to

see how he is. I'll be the only one not there. How can we be a team if one of us is missing?"

We head back toward school.

Sam finally says, "You won't be the only one missing."

"What do you mean?"

He starts running again. "I'm not going. We can hang at school together instead if you want."

I'm shocked. "Why wouldn't you go?"

He darts left into the woods that'll lead us back to school. It's just like him to sneak in a run on the course. Reluctantly, I follow.

"Sam?"

"You don't get it, do you?"

Apparently not. I don't get anything anymore.

"Look at me. Do you really think Bobby and his dad are the only ones who think I'm the enemy? Bobby might be the one that hit me, or the one saying things out loud, but the stares I get from other people are just as bad. Even Matt and Rigo ignore me. It's all day. Everywhere I go. Man, sometimes you're so blind."

It's not that I haven't noticed, but those kids are just being punks. I never thought it would bother Sam, but if it does, why hasn't he said anything to me before?

"Are you sure you're not just paranoid? Besides, I doubt that Kirk would think anything bad about you."

"Get your head out of the mud. You're so clueless

sometimes. Nothing's the same anymore; not school, not home, not even cross country. Probably not even Kirk."

Sam keeps running, but I stop.

He's wrong. He's got to show up tomorrow, especially if he thinks people see him as the enemy. Showing up will prove to everyone that he's just Sam. I lace my hands on my head and pace. So what if everything is different? It doesn't mean he and I can't stay the same. I haven't changed, and he doesn't have to, either.

I turn to take a short cut out of the woods and run smack into the giant web of a Golden Silk spider. No matter how much I pull, pieces of the web stick to my hair, face, and chest. My fingers just tangle it more.

Seriously, I hate cross country.

CHAPTER 12

....

I'm already awake when Mom walks into my room holding a hanger with a pair of pants, a button down shirt,
and a tie wrapped around the top. "Thought you might
need this for the funeral," she says.

I hop out of bed. "You changed your mind?"

"It's not going to be easy, but if Kirk's your friend,
then you should be there." She exhales and something about her sudden posture and voice make me
think she's trying to be strong even though I can tell
she's a wreck. "Look, funerals are hard. If you change
your mind, or even want to leave once we're there,
that's fine."

I hug her. "Thank you."

"Get dressed. Breakfast will be ready in a few minutes."

....

Mom pulls into the Star of David Memorial Gardens Cemetery. Her fingers are white-knuckled around the steering wheel and she hasn't said a word during the whole drive. She parks but doesn't get out of the car, even though people are pouring into the chapel already. I don't want to blow it by saying anything, so I wait next to her, as patient as I can.

After a few minutes, she opens her door. "We should go in."

I nod.

Uncle Hugh and Aunt Margie are waiting for us near the front door. Aunt Margie gives Mom a hug and it sets her off. The tears are like the rain bands of a hurricane, fast and hard, and she backs away. "I can't. I'm sorry, I just can't."

Please don't do this. Not now. I want to see Kirk and make sure he's okay. I look from Mom to Uncle Hugh and back.

Aunt Margie pats Uncle Hugh's arm. "Why don't you take Jake in? Olivia and I will sit in the car until it's over." She leads Mom away from the entrance.

Uncle Hugh and I go inside. A man in a suit hands me a small black beanie thing to put on my head. I want to tell him I'm not Jewish and I don't need to wear one—kind of like my friends who can't take Communion at my church if they're not Catholic—but I look around and all the guys are wearing them, even ones I know aren't Jewish, so I take it and put it on. I tug it tight, but it doesn't fit well. It just sort of sits on top of my hair. The entrance to the chapel is packed, so I peek in and see Coach Rehart motioning for me to come over. Uncle Hugh nods that it's okay and I go sit next to one of the seventh graders while pushing the cap down on my head again—praying that the thing doesn't fall off. Sam's nowhere to be seen. If he's so concerned about people thinking he's the enemy, this definitely doesn't help.

The chapel is dark and gray. There's a wood coffin up front next to a small black podium. A single window above lets in a bit of light. A man wearing a scarf—the rabbi—comes into the room from a side door. Kirk's family is behind him and they walk to the front row and sit. Some of the women are wearing dark sunglasses and I wonder if it's to hide their puffy eyes. Kirk's not hiding his, though. Everyone can see he's been crying. It makes my own eyes sting.

The rabbi reads from a book and then invites some man up to talk about Mr. Steiner. It must be his brother, because he tells a funny story about when they were kids and they dared each other to swim across the canal where they'd seen a gator the day before. Both of them did it, though Mr. Steiner swam so fast he lost his bathing suit. Everyone laughs—even Kirk.

One of Kirk's little sisters gets up next. She talks about how their dog Boo died last year and now Boo's probably happy because she and Mr. Steiner are together again. I look at the ceiling, begging myself not to cry.

Kirk's next. His hands are shoved deep in his pockets. All of a sudden, I wish I had Grandpa's medal with me.

Kirk takes a deep breath. "When I was little, my dad wasn't home much. When he was, everyone wanted to be with him. He was *that* great. But I wanted time with him alone so, when I was about five, I started following him when he went out to run every morning. The sun was hardly ever up and it was nice to have my dad to myself while everyone else slept. It became our thing. I loved it, and I became a pretty good runner because of it."

My stomach lobs. I hated Kirk for being so fast, but now I feel bad.

"He never saw me race but always checked in to see how I did after one." He sniffles. "My dad was a hero. Not because he was in the Navy and fought battles. Not because he worked hard and earned the rank of a lieutenant. He was a hero just because he was my dad."

A lump the size of a cannonball forms in my throat.

"He was a hero because he did his time and he was

finally coming home to be with us. He wanted to see me race. I waited my whole life for that." He wipes away a tear, then another, until he has to stop talking because his voice is shaking so much.

I quickly brush my own tears away. I get how Kirk feels because Dad never sees me race either, but at least we still have time to change that.

I can tell Kirk's trying to be brave when he takes a breath and keeps going. "I'll never have that chance now and as mad as that makes me . . ." He stops again and looks at the coffin like he's talking right to his dad. "I know he was going to give up something he loved for me. I love you, Dad." He plods back to his seat, slumps over, and buries his face in his hands.

I wipe my runny nose on my sleeve and close my eyes. I wish Dad would do that for me—that he'd see what happened with Mr. Steiner and realize he should want to be home more.

The rabbi thanks everyone for coming and invites us all to the burial site out front. Suddenly there are a lot of people moving and six people line up, three on each side of the coffin. Kirk's one of them, and they slowly walk it out of the chapel.

Outside, two people—both in Navy uniform— drape an American flag over the casket, then we all head to the gravesite. No one talks; we just walk in the heat, shaded every few steps by a random tree. Sweat drips down my back. I can see the air conditioning in the car blowing Mom's hair as I pass by. I give her a small wave and she half-smiles back.

Mr. Steiner's body is wheeled over to a stone wall where he's going to be buried inside one of the squares. The door's open—waiting for him. The family sits on a bench in front, surrounded by a crowd so big I can't get close enough to see or hear anything the rabbi's saying.

All of a sudden, I hear gunshots behind me. I duck as my heart races and some people run for cover. Before I can think, there's another round, and then one more. I should've known there would be a gun salute. I feel dumb, but people around me are holding their chests and breathing heavy, too. It doesn't look like anyone was expecting it.

I relax a little and watch, knowing what comes next. Sam would have loved to see this. A single bugler steps out and "Taps" echoes across the field of tombstones. Chills prick my neck and arms, and I fight the stinging in my eyes again. When the bugler's done, the two uniformed people fold the flag that was draped over Mr. Steiner's casket. They place three bullet casings inside, tuck the final flap, and one marches in perfect rhythm over to Kirk, handing it to him. I picture Mom, at my age, sitting on a bench getting her dad's flag after his funeral. My heart skips as I struggle to breathe. There were times when I'd imagined attending a funeral like this before—how neat I thought that would be. But now, my stomach squeezes in on itself knowing that it's over. That even though Mr. Steiner and Grandpa fought and died for their country, they're never coming back. It doesn't seem as cool anymore.

....

I waited in a long line to talk to Kirk after the service, but he gave up about halfway through and ducked off into a limo. I don't blame him. I mean, how many I'm-so-sorrys can you take? It doesn't change anything.

Uncle Hugh took us to lunch after and Mom was in a better mood thanks to Aunt Margie. On our way home, as Mom and I come around the corner into our neighborhood, we spot a big black SUV and three cop cars in front of Sam's house.

"Stop!" I yell.

Mom says, "Is that the FBI?" She slows but doesn't stop. Two men are wearing vests that clearly say FBI and they are handing some papers to Mr. Madina. He and Sam stare at them before one of the cops cuffs Mr. Madina.

"Mom, you have to pull over! This can't be right."

She looks at me sternly. "We can't get involved. He's obviously done something wrong. They wouldn't cuff him for no reason."

But they must've got something mixed up. They don't know Mr. Madina like I do.

Sam's mom stands like a stone statue in the front yard—eyes wide and lips clenched, but not fighting for them to leave her husband alone. The little American flags thrash in the wind as Mr. Madina's led to the cop car. It's like I'm watching a scene on TV—a scene so fake that Sam and I would look at each other and laugh because it would never happen in real life.

Neighbors are outside of their houses, all staring. Then I notice that Bobby's front and center, taking it all in, as Mr. Madina ducks his head when they stuff him into the back of the cruiser.

We're almost past their house now. I throw my palm against the window while my other hand grabs the door handle. Just then, Sam looks at me. I turn to look at Mom. Mom looks at the road ahead. I shove the car door open and jump out. I hear tires screeching to a stop.

Mom yells, "Get back in here right now!"

But I'm already at Sam's side.

He hollers at the cops. "We're Americans! Look!" He waves my grandpa's medal in the air.

"Yeah!" I belt. "We're all Americans!"

The cops don't even look back.

Aamber wraps her arm around her mom, but Mrs. Madina must be in shock. Sam's jaw is clenched and his fists are balled tight. As the police cruiser hauls Mr. Madina away, Sam runs to the edge of his yard, picks up a rock, then hurls it at the fading cop car before he drops to his knees and cries. He's the second friend I've seen lose it today, only this time, I can try to help.

Bobby claps and tries to get the crowd fired up. He shouts, "Finally, they're cleaning up the neighborhood!"

No one joins him, but no one helps the Madinas, either. Not even Mom, who's still in the car. How can she just sit there and do *nothing*?

I pull Sam to his feet and herd the Madinas inside so people will stop staring at them. I catch Sam's eye. It's clear he's raging inside. He and I take Mrs. Madina by the arms to keep her from falling over as she stumbles toward the house.

Sam's got the papers from the FBI in his hand but still manages to shove the front door open so hard that the knob makes a hole in the drywall. "It's not fair! He didn't do anything!" he screams.

And I agree. Mr. Madina's the most honest man I know. One time, Sam and I paid a kid to do our science fair project and after we got an A, Mr. Madina took us out to celebrate. Only he knew we had cheated and everything blew up over a hot fudge sundae. Sam's dad gave us an ultimatum: we could either tell the teacher or he would. So, no, he'd never help a terrorist. He's just too good.

Mrs. Madina's like dead weight, but somehow we get her to the couch while Aamber goes to make some tea.

I turn to Sam. "They won't keep him. They wouldn't do that. I mean, they have no reason, right?"

He crumbles up the papers and throws them on the coffee table. "He didn't do anything wrong."

"I know. It'll be okay."

Sam doesn't talk again. He just stares at me, and I feel stupid because it's not okay. Nothing's okay. And we both know it.

Outside, a horn honks. I walk to the window and look toward the corner where our car's parked. Mom's flapping her arms like a crazy lady for me to come out, but that's not what gets me riled. Off to the side, Bobby's pulling the flags out of Sam's yard and it's obvious he's looking for a fight again. I'll show him who's garbage.

Crash. Aamber dropped something in the kitchen and Sam jumps. As he walks toward her, I bolt for the front door, yelling over my shoulder, "I'll call you later!"

I don't know if he hears me or not because I'm out the door in a flash and lunge for Bobby. I wrangle the flags from his hand before he shoves me to the ground and pins me.

Mom rushes over. "Get off him!"

Bobby hops up, grabs his bike, and takes off faster than a soldier in retreat. Chicken.

When Mom offers me her hand, I blow her off and stand on my own. I don't want her anywhere near me.

I'm about to put the flags back in the ground when I see Sam staring out the front window. He looks at me holding the flags and his eyes bug out—like he thinks I pulled them out.

"No, Sam—" It's too late. The curtain falls back over the window.

I make a dash for the steps, but Mom stops me. "Jake Daniel! What are you doing attacking Bobby again? Get in the car!"

"I need to talk to Sam."

She straightens and her nostrils flare. "I *said* get in the car!"

Mom's only screamed at me once that I can remember. It was last year when I told a joke I guess I didn't really understand and apparently it had some twisted meaning. She scared me then and she's scaring me now, but it doesn't make me hate her any less at this moment. I storm over to the car and slam the door.

She turns the key. "I didn't want to be right about Adil, but . . ."

"He was just doing his job!" I spit the words. "So what if Atta had a bank account there? What if he called Dad up and asked him how to work some software and Dad helped him? Would that mean Dad's bad, too?"

We're home in less than thirty seconds. "It's not the same. They'd never question your father."

"You're not serious, right?"

"Things aren't always cut and dry, Jake. They're just not. I asked you to stay away from Sam, and I mean it. Especially now."

My mouth hangs open, and I'm glued to the seat. She's a traitor. Worse than Benedict Arnold. I can't even wrap my brain around what she's saying. I have to call Dad. I have to get away from her. I run into the house, grab the cordless phone, and then lock myself in my room.

My fingers fumble over the buttons as I dial Dad's cell.

A few seconds later, he answers. "Hello?"

The tightness in my chest makes it hard to breathe, but I spill out everything that happened today, including the comment Mom made about the FBI. My stomach tightens just saying it.

Dad sighs. "Listen, what your Mom said isn't true.

If I'd been the one working at the bank, the FBI would definitely have questioned me, too. And if they found something, they'd arrest me for sure. Mom's not thinking straight right now, but she's right that they wouldn't take Mr. Madina without a reason."

"So, you think he did something? You think he's involved?"

"I don't know. I . . ." Dad pauses. "I mean, I've known Adil for years." He exhales sharply. "My gut says no, he didn't do anything. But . . ."

My tongue feels extra big in my mouth, but I have to ask. I have to know. "But, what?"

"But, I guess we just don't know the facts right now. Let me see if I can find anything out. We owe the Madinas that much."

Yeah, we do. They're practically family. The FBI's full of smart people, but this time, they must've made a mistake.

"Look, I know you're upset with Mom, but I still need you to check on her, okay? The funeral couldn't have been easy on her."

It wasn't *easy* for anybody.

"Good luck at your meet tomorrow. Wish I could be there."

I wonder how many times Mr. Steiner said those same words to Kirk.

"I'll be home Thursday afternoon. Love you." And he hangs up.

That leaves two days of pretty much total silence in our house because I don't plan to say a word to Mom. Dad's giving Mr. Madina the benefit of the doubt, but Mom's already convinced he did something. So much for innocent until proven guilty.

CHAPTER 13
September 19, 2001
Wednesday

....

Sam wouldn't answer the phone last night, so I head over early to talk to him before school.

Aamber answers the door in a bathrobe. Her eyes are swollen. "Hey."

It's awkward because I feel bad for her, but it's not like we've ever been friends and I don't really know how to make her feel better, so I just say, "I came to see if you guys are okay."

She shrugs. "We're still trying to figure out where they took my dad. Someone's got to know."

It didn't hit me before, but maybe Uncle Hugh could help. He knows just about everyone in town. "I'm sure they'll bring him back today. Is Sam ready to go?"

She scrunches her long hair in a ball and wraps a rubber band around it on top of her head. "Neither of us are going to school today."

"But we have the biggest meet of the year." I feel horrible as soon as I say it. Sometimes I'm pretty dumb. Sam definitely has bigger problems than Palmetto, but I guess I hoped he'd still race anyway.

"Yeah, tell Coach Rehart what happened, okay?"

"I'm sorry. I didn't mean . . ." To be so dumb? Selfish? Idiotic? All of the above? I have to get out of here before I make it worse. "Tell him to call me later."

"Sure." She reaches for something on the table next to the door inside and hands me back Grandpa's medal and all my other stuff. "He told me to give this to you."

"Thanks."

"See ya." She closes the door.

I doubt Coach will take the news any better than I did. We need Sam to run. To win. Besides, I'm pretty sure Mr. Madina would want him to race today.

....

The front of the school is packed with kids. Kirk gets out of his mom's car looking pretty strong. I'm surprised he's even here, but he's got his Mangrove jersey on. How's he going to run? How will he just go back to normal? But deep down,

I know he's doing it for his dad. If he can run when he just buried his dad yesterday, Sam should be able to run, too.

Kirk passes me. "Hey."

"Wait up." I run a few steps to catch him. "I tried to talk to you after the funeral yesterday but you left. Not that I blame you. I would have, too."

"Thanks for being there. I saw the team. It was nice of you guys to come."

"Are you okay? You sure you want to race today?"

He stops at his locker. It could just be the lighting, but his eyes look watery. "My dad was the ultimate team player. 'Honor, Courage, Commitment.' He lived by that and he'd want me to, too. I have to run today—for him and for the team."

"I don't think Sam's coming today so it'll be a tough meet."

"I didn't see him at the funeral yesterday. Is he sick?"

I don't even know how to explain why Sam skipped yesterday. After seeing how many people stood in the street and watched Mr. Madina get hauled off without helping, I realize there are more people like Bobby in our town than I thought.

Kirk shakes me. "Hello?"

"Sorry." Better to know where he stands. "He, uh, he's not sick. He just didn't think you'd want him there."

"That's stupid. Why not?"

My hand loosens on my backpack and I exhale, not realizing I'd even been holding my breath. I spill the details about Bobby and Mr. Madina. I tell him how Sam thought Kirk might not have wanted him to show up at the funeral because he was Muslim, like the terrorists who killed his dad.

The first bell blares and we walk down the hallway. Kirk's expression is totally blank. Finally, all he says is, "The FBI took Sam's dad?" He shakes his head before he turns and heads to his homeroom.

I have no idea if he feels bad about Sam's dad or if he believes Mr. Madina actually did something wrong. I go through people in my head, tallying up who might think Mr. Madina's one of the enemies and who doesn't. Mom, the FBI, and Bobby all think he did something wrong. Dad seems neutral. Sam's definitely on his dad's side. Kirk, well, I have no idea after his last comment. I need to find out who my and Sam's allies are.

....

There's an awkward silence in the locker room when Kirk comes in. Most of the team stares as he makes his way to the bench. When he passes me, I put my hand in the air. He high-fives me and the tension's gone as quick as it came. The team circles in and welcomes him back.

When they're done, Kirk says to me, "I wish Sam were here to run, but I think he's right to stay home with his mom." He sits and changes his shoes. "I'll try to talk to him later and see if he's okay. It looks like it's up to you and me to win this race, though."

I smile wide, happier than ever that Kirk's on our side, and I don't just mean for cross country. "We got this," I tell him. And I'm excited to see Tyler. To finally get my revenge. I take Grandpa's medal from my pants pocket, look at it for a second, and place it extra carefully in my bag. My neck tenses when I feel someone watching me.

Bobby's eyes dart from my bag to me. He's standing at the end of the row of lockers with Rigo and a few other kids behind him. "Here he is."

The guys from the team must sense something because they stand guard behind me.

I straighten. "Here I am. So, what?"

Bobby struts down the aisle. "These guys came to watch you get pantsed again. I told them all about last year, but they didn't believe me. Did they, Rigo?"

Rigo laughs and shakes his head. "No."

My face is hot. Sweat breaks out across my forehead. My secret's out. How does he know? "You're making stuff up. I told you what happened."

"Yeah, well, half the Palmetto team says what a skinny white butt you have."

Bobby's friends crack up. I want to run, but I can't. I can't let Bobby win.

Bobby pulls at his shirt. "So, we're here to watch it live. I hope you're ready, loser."

Without thinking, I lunge at him. He might be bigger than me, but I shove him right into a locker then cock my arm, ready to strike. Coach pulls me off and hollers for everyone to get out.

He's got the back of my shirt wadded in his hand and drags me away as Bobby stands there, laughing at me. My arms swing wildly, begging for a piece of him as I'm dragged to Coach's office.

He drops me into one of his chairs, then closes the door. "That's twice in one week, Jake. It doesn't bode well."

"He starts it every time!" My face is still hot with anger, and embarrassment.

Coach slams his fist onto his desk. "It doesn't matter. You need to find a way to make your statement without throwing punches. You hear me?"

I hear him, but I don't agree, so I say nothing.

He calms down and then sits behind his desk, which is strewn with random bunches of paper. "Why do you think I make you run cross country?"

Because you like to torture me.

Maybe he realizes I'm not going to reply because he says, "Cross country is a sport that makes you think. There's a strategy to running a race, and you have to play it smart. There's no straight shot to the finish line and you've got to be ready for whatever comes your way. I know you prefer track, but think about what I've said. You need to master the concept of cross country and apply it elsewhere in your life."

Master the concept of cross country? He's crazy. I don't want to run it in the first place, so why would I want to master it?

He sighs loudly. "Maybe this will get your attention then. You put your team in a real bad spot out in the locker room, because I can't let you run today."

I spring from my seat. "What? It's the biggest race of the year!"

"You should have thought of that before you went after Bobby."

"You can't be serious. Come on! I never even got to hit him."

"Oh, I'm serious." He runs his fingers through his hair. "I just hate to break it to the rest of the team. They were definitely counting on you."

"I'll sit out the next meet, then. I'll clean the school toilets. Anything! But you've gotta let me race."

"Sorry, kid. There's a much bigger picture here, and you need to see it."

Yeah, there's a bigger picture, for sure. Bobby gets away with this again, and now Tyler will, too. Nothing's fair anymore.

I get up to go grab my stuff. It's not like I'm going to stay and celebrate Palmetto's victory, that's for sure.

Coach steps in front of the door. "Where do you think you're going?"

"Home." I try to get around him.

"You're still part of this team, and you're required to be here this afternoon." He hands me a clipboard and the stopwatch from around his neck. "You can log times at the finish line."

I don't take the clipboard. "I have a headache. Can't I just see you at practice tomorrow?"

"Nope." He spins me toward the door. "If you want to continue to be part of this team, you better get out there and keep time."

I shake my shoulders from his hands. I'm not sure I want to be part of the team anymore. I head into the locker room and Kirk's waiting for me on a bench.

He says, "Is it true? Is that why you're so mad at Tyler?"

I ignore him and yank my bag from my locker. There's no reason to admit it out loud.

He stands. "You leaving?"

"Coach benched me and I'm not going to stick around and watch us lose or watch Tyler win again."

"Who says we're going to lose?"

He's as crazy as Coach Rehart. Without Sam and me running, our team doesn't stand a chance. Kirk's lightning-fast, but he's only one in the whole lineup. I look at him, ready to tell him he's nuts, but when I see his face, I remember the funeral. I remember Kirk's words and how he's running for his dad, and I know he needs this today.

I flop onto the bench and suck in a deep breath.

He stares at me, so I swipe his head with my fingers. "Fine, but you don't stand a chance if someone doesn't light a fire under those seventh graders." I get up and shove my bag back in my locker.

His eyes look like they're smiling. "Then you better get out there with some matches." He sticks out his fist.

I bump it.

....

The team is stretching out and Coach pats me on the back as I take the clipboard and stopwatch from him. When Kirk sees his mom, he breaks from the group to go over to her.

I quickly get everyone's attention and huddle them in. "Listen, you guys were all at the funeral yesterday. You know how important this race is for Kirk, right?"

They nod.

"I'm sorry Coach won't let me run today." I look at him and he shakes his head, but I could swear he's kind of smiling, too. "And you can see that Sam's not here, but it doesn't mean you guys can quit."

As I talk, Palmetto's team heads toward the starting line. Tyler waves at me and smirks; I want to tie his shoes together and dangle him from a tree. This is all Bobby's fault. Out of the corner of my eye, Mrs. Steiner kisses Kirk on the forehead and he's about to head back over to us.

"Kirk's running this for his dad. You should run it for Kirk. It means everything to him and the team has to stick together. You got this."

Coach nods at me and Kirk's back in the circle now. When we raise our hands in the air, Kirk's captain armband shines in the sun, and I hope it'll bring him luck.

"Mangrove on three," I yell. "One, two, three."

"Mangrove!"

The team scatters to the starting line. Tyler sees me walk away from the start and even though the gun's about to sound, he runs over to me. "Wow, too scared to run against me, Jakey?"

My blood's like lava rushing through my veins. Instantly, I start limping. "Nope, just an injury, but you're going down next time. I hope you're ready."

He laughs. "Right, an injury. That's pretty convenient. It won't be as fun winning today knowing you're on the sideline, but I'll take it. See ya next time."

The gun goes off and so do the runners. I calculate in my head how I can stick to my plan: dump water on Tyler in the woods and still make it back to the finish line for scoring without Coach noticing. I could run straight across the field and catch Tyler near the halfway mark. I'm already looking around for a cup as the plan unfolds in my head. I rush over to the water cooler and am just about to dart for the woods when I hear, "Is something wrong?" Mom's standing at the fence, eyes all puzzled.

I thought Mom might be too upset about everything to even show up today, but I should've known better. The last thing I need is her going off the deep end about the whole Bobby situation. So I lie. "It's just a pulled muscle from not running enough these last few days. I'll be fine by tomorrow."

"I'm glad it's nothing serious." She's totally buying it. "We'll put a heating pad on it when we get home."

I want her out of here quick, just in case someone tips her off about the locker room scene. "You can go if you want. I'm just going to keep stats at the finish line and I'll walk home."

"I have a book in the car so I'll just wait there for you to finish." She walks toward the parking lot.

I tug on the stopwatch around my neck as I head to the finish chute. There's no time now to pull my prank on Tyler, but I consider myself lucky to have avoided a Mom-bomb.

Then I hear it. The unmistakable voice of Coach calling out, "Mrs. Green."

No. He wouldn't, right? This was between me and him. Mom's mouth gapes and her face is redder than a lit fuse as Coach speaks with her—presumably spilling the beans about what happened in the locker room. The bomb's about to explode. She turns and motions me over. I look at Coach. He nods. I straighten as I walk over to them because, honestly, I haven't done anything wrong. My only regret is that Coach saw me shove Bobby and benched me. Mom can be as mad as she wants.

Coach takes the clipboard and stopwatch from me as Mom says, "Get your stuff from the locker room and get in the car."

"But—"

Her eyes narrow, though she keeps her voice calm. "Now."

I look at both of them, then storm off. This is so unfair.

....

Mom shuts the radio off when I get in the car. "What has gotten into you? It's like all of the sudden you want to be everyone's hero."

I was expecting a lecture, but this doesn't make sense. Since when does defending myself make me want to be a hero? "What are you *talking* about?" It comes out way ruder than I mean, and I know it won't help my case.

She looks at me as if I shoved her and not Bobby. "Do *not* take that tone with me. Do you understand?"

I nod.

"Mr. Rehart told me you got into it with Bobby again. Just because Bobby has an issue with Sam does not mean you need to keep sticking your nose in that business."

I grip my knee and will myself not to yell at her. "This has nothing to do with Sam. Why would you even think that? Bobby started in on me about the Palmetto meet last year so I shoved him. That's it. No big deal."

She bites her lip for just a second and closes her eyes. I hope she feels bad for assuming wrong. When she opens her eyes, she says, "It *is* a big deal. Big enough to get you suspended from running, remember? And big enough that I have to keep you home from school until you realize that you can't go around physically retaliating on people the way you're so fond of lately. No TV, no cross country, nothing."

I lurch forward in my seat. "You're joking."

"I can't trust you anymore. Until you can let this stuff with Bobby go, I'm going to have to keep a closer eye on you. You're embarrassing yourself and your family every time you fight this kid. We didn't raise you that way."

I sink into the small space between the door and the seat, pressing the back of my head against the car window. There's no point in talking to her. It's like we're total strangers. I'm still Jake, but she's not the same Mom.

....

Mom's in her room, and I need to talk to Sam.

"Hello?" He answers the phone, almost breathless.

"Hey."

I hear the letdown in his voice. "Oh . . . hi."

He obviously didn't check the caller ID. It sounds like he hoped I was someone else. "Any news on your dad?"

"Nothing."

"Are you all okay?" Of course they're not okay, and I know it, but I can't think of what to say for the first time since we've been friends. Why is everything so awkward between us lately?

"Do you really have to ask that?"

"No. I . . ." I stumble over my words. "I mean, it was dumb, but I feel bad and I want to make sure your mom's alright. She didn't look good yesterday."

"She's not alright. She hasn't come out of her room since they took my dad away. We made like a hundred phone calls trying to get answers."

"Listen, about the flag thing yesterday. I wasn't taking them out of your yard. I was putting them back in. You know that, right?"

"Whatever. It doesn't even matter."

It does to me. I need him to believe me, to ask me for help and partner up so we can find out what's going on with his dad, knock Bobby's brains around until he sees right again, and get back to cross country where Sam can lead the team like he's supposed to.

"Yeah, well, I wanted you to know." I flop onto my desk chair and see the Dolphins tickets pinned to my cork board. I forgot all about the upcoming game. I run my finger over the section information: nose bleed seats. It's going to sound like another stupid question, but I have to know. "The Dolphin game's this weekend. Your dad's gone and all, but do you think you'll still go with me?" I remember how excited Sam was when Mom told him one ticket was for him. Two weeks ago,

I'd have never dreamed there was a shot Sam wouldn't go, but now I hold my breath as I wait for him to answer.

"No, I don't think I can." He pauses for a moment. "I went to check out that mosque today."

"What does that have to do with the Dolphin game?" And why would he even want to learn about Muslims at a time like this?

"On Sunday, we're having a meeting there. The sheikh—that's the guy in charge—said we should come up with some ideas on how we can get people to understand Islam so they don't associate us with those terrorists."

My arm's weak as I hold the phone. *Us.* Sam said it like he's already one of them. How's he getting sucked into this after only one trip there? "How are you going to help them teach other people about Islam when you don't even know anything about it?"

"I know more than you think. My grandparents are Muslim, remember?"

I wonder how much he actually knows. I wonder why he's kept it all from me until now. I thought we were best friends. He knows every little thing about me, but lately, he's practically a stranger. I don't want to argue with him, though. We need to stick together. "Yeah, I remember. Look, I have homework. I'll see you tomorrow?" Maybe things will be better when we walk to school—if I can convince Mom to let me go.

"I'm staying home again. My mom needs me here."

He's right, and I can't be mad about that, but I hope once we see each other again, things will go back to normal between us. "Okay, I'll try to stop by tomorrow."

I wait for him to say *Great!* Or, *Cool.* Something good.

Instead, all he says is, "I don't know. Maybe." And then he hangs up on me.

CHAPTER 14
SEPTEMBER 20, 2001
THURSDAY

....

Mom keeps me out of school because of the fight with Bobby, but I don't get to sleep in and hang at home all day. Nope. She's taking me to work with her, like I'm four. I feel like a prisoner.

Uncle Hugh laughs and wraps me in his usual bear hug when I walk in the office. "Jake, you playing hooky?"

I don't know how to answer him. Mom might be too embarrassed to admit that I got in a fight—even if it was for a good reason—so I laugh with him and don't say anything, letting his strong arms squeeze me for a solid twenty seconds.

But Mom can't lie, especially to Uncle Hugh. He's

like her dad. "Jake got in trouble at school. He's being punished."

He releases me from his grip. "You? I don't believe that." He turns to Mom. "This is one fine boy, Olivia. I'm sure it's all a misunderstanding."

I think he's waiting for an explanation and I'm all set to give him one. I'll tell him about *all* the misunderstandings, including the Madinas and Mom. I open my mouth, ready to fire away, but Mom grabs my shoulders and leads me to the conference room, calling over her shoulder, "His coach didn't think so, and now Jake has to accept my consequences. You don't mind that he's here, do you?"

"Of course not. I have an unexpected schedule change and have to go to a city meeting for a few hours. I know Gabe Ryan's supposed to come by. Can you meet with him and give him the numbers we ran?"

"Of course." She hurries behind her desk and checks the calendar, leaving me in the conference room alone.

I was set to ask Uncle Hugh to help find out where Sam's dad is, but if he leaves, I might be able to just slip into his office and find the information myself, without Mom even knowing. If we can get Mr. Madina back, maybe Sam will snap out of whatever crazy mode he's in and this will all be just a drop of water, as Grandma would say.

I pretend to be studious and prop my math book upright, hiding the sheet I'm scribbling my to-do list on:

1. Fix things with Sam.
2. Help find Mr. Madina and clear his name.
3. Run three miles today.

Mom sticks her head in the doorway and I act like I'm in deep in thought over a math problem.

She says, "Honey, I need you to finish up at my desk. I have a meeting in here in fifteen minutes for a fundraiser Uncle Hugh and I are working on."

I can't hide the smile that's taken over my face. This is too easy.

She must notice my mood change because she says, "That doesn't mean you can goof off. You still have schoolwork to finish."

"Right." I try to sound upset, but I'd never win an award for acting.

I grab my stuff and plunk down on Mom's leather swivel chair. When I was a kid, I used to love spinning on it till the whole room seemed like it was upside down. Then I'd get up and try to walk and end up bumping into the walls. Uncle Hugh thought it was the funniest thing. I don't spin myself now, though. Instead, I shake the mouse and hope Mom's computer screen lights up. It doesn't. This just means I'll have to raid Uncle Hugh's office once Mom's meeting starts.

A man in khaki pants and a short sleeve shirt with

bright yellow school buses all over it enters the office. No matter how old I get, I swear I will never wear a shirt like that.

They greet each other like old friends, and she leads him to the conference room. When she comes back, she grabs a piece of tape and hangs a sign on the entrance door to the office building: In a meeting. Please come back in an hour. Then she flips the lock—securing me in her mom-made jail cell.

She takes a tray of cookies with her, and before she shuts the door she whispers, "Do your work, and don't touch my computer."

I won't touch her computer, but I don't promise not to touch Uncle Hugh's. I have no idea how long the meeting will last so I move quickly once the door to the conference room clicks shut. I slip down the hall to Uncle Hugh's big office. Wooden plaques, certificates, and photos cover all four walls. The photo of my family with Uncle Hugh and Aunt Margie is staring at me and I suddenly feel guilty for my invasion of his space, but I have to do this—for Sam. Luckily, the computer is on, but I have no clue where to begin. I doubt there will be a folder labeled Mr. Madina: prisoner. There's a picture of a screen that says My Computer and my shaky fingers click on it, then I see a file folder that's labeled Important Documents. Could that be it? I slide the mouse over—

"Jake Daniel Green!" Mom's throws her hands on her hips and she's whispering but screaming at the same time. "What do you think you're doing?"

No point in lying. Besides chaining me to my bed, there's not much she can do to keep me from helping my friend. "Looking for information about Mr. Madina."

"I warned you to leave that alone and to stay away from Sam. I won't tell you again." Still shouting at me with her eyes, she motions me back to her desk.

I'm starting to see why some kids say they hate their parents.

She hunkers over me as I slouch in her chair. "I don't even know what to do with you anymore. You disobey me every chance you get. It's got to stop."

She straightens. "Now, I'm going back in that meeting, but I'll be keeping the door cracked. If you so much as move from that chair, you'll be . . ."

I wait for her threat, but it doesn't come. There's nothing else to take away. We're stuck in this circle of right versus wrong. Only she can't see that she's the one who's wrong.

....

Mom and I tiptoe around each other like soldiers on a field of landmines the rest of the day. Dad should be home any second, and I decide to wait for him on the front porch.

His car pulls up a few minutes later. "Hey, champ."

"Hi."

"You doing okay?"

I shrug.

"I heard what happened yesterday before the meet."

Of course he did. "Did Mom also tell you she's taking everything in my life away from me for no reason? She's being so unfair."

He sits in the rocker and looks like he's trying to find the right words. Finally he says, "I'm going to take next week off. Your mom needs me right now."

Mom needs him? What about me? I needed him last week. I begged him not to go, but he said he had to. Now he'll stay home for Mom. I stand. I have to get out of here.

He tugs my arm. "Jake, wait . . ."

"I need to get my practice run in. I'll be back later." I make a mad-dash for the pavement—smooth and safe.

I run under clouds that look like they might burst and past the Wilkeys' house. I glare at the window and swear I see a shadow behind the sheer curtain, which is odd because their darker curtains are usually closed tight. Do they even know what people say about them? Do they care? I mean, if the whole neighborhood is wrong about them, why don't they want to come out and prove they're normal? And Sam . . . why is he going to a mosque instead of trying to prove he and his family are innocent? I wish my brain had an off button.

I pass the school and then spot Sam out front of the mosque down the street. He doesn't see me but I watch him for a few minutes as he talks to a group of kids that look like they're in high school. This is crazy. He should be at practice.

On my way back home, I see Aamber sitting on her front porch swing so I stop. She's eating a Pop-Tart and for a second we both just stare at each other, not sure if we should say hi or what because it's not like we ever do. She finally gives me a half-wave, so I head up the steps.

"Any word about your dad?"

She shakes her head and hands me a corner of her cherry Pop-Tart.

I don't really like Pop-Tarts but stick it in my mouth anyway, buying time till I figure out what else to say. I sit next to her on the big swing, chewing slowly.

She pushes the ground with her feet and we rock back and forth. "If it makes you feel better, Sam's shutting me out, too. He's just mad at the world right now, but he'll calm down."

I get that. I do. Some whacked out guys killed thousands of people and managed to screw up the lives of thousands more. For what? They're dead, but we're stuck dealing with the mess. Sam's mad at the world. So am I. Still, it's no reason for him to blow me off. I don't want to talk about him though, not now. So instead I ask, "Is your mom doing okay?"

Aamber rests her head on the back of the swing so she's looking up at the wooden-slatted porch ceiling and says, "It's like she's in a coma or something. If I weren't spoon-feeding her, she wouldn't even eat."

"Is anyone helping you? I mean, how are you getting food and stuff?"

"Come on, you know my mom's always had a mini-grocery store in our pantry. We're stocked for a year or so." She laughs and I do too, because, for a second, everything feels normal again. Well, except for the fact that Aamber and I are actually getting along and having a conversation.

I don't want to wreck the moment by saying something dumb, or saying anything really, so we just sit there, quiet and peaceful for a long time.

Eventually, she stands. "I should get back inside and check on her."

I stand, too. Part of me wants to say thanks for fifteen minutes of normalcy because that's what I feel—especially knowing I have to go home to my parents now.

"Hope she's better soon. And I hope you hear something about your dad."

She closes the door and the orange curtain on the inside of it sways so I can't watch her walk away.

I run across her yard and round the corner to the Wilkeys'. A green Gatorade sits on the bottom porch step. I stop. I'm not working in their yard today, so why is the bottle outside? I look at the window and the shadow is still there. I'm almost home and definitely don't need the drink, so I run past it and don't look back.

....

Dad knocks on my door and then pushes it open. "The president is about to make a speech. Thought you might like to watch."

I bounce off my bed and head out the door.

As I pass my parents' room, I see Mom propped in bed, eyes fixed on the wall in front of her. For some reason, she looks small, and for a second I feel bad for her.

I sink into the couch and Dad clicks the remote. President Bush is standing in front of Congress in one of the rooms of the Capitol. The crowd gives him a standing ovation before he even begins talking. He starts his speech by saying he's seen the state of the union and how good it is because everyone's been strong. Things may be different in Washington, but hardly anyone's been strong here. Everyone in that room is on their feet again, cheering loudly. He goes on, saying that countries across the world have shown support in our favor by playing our national anthem overseas and taking moments of silence on our behalf.

When President Bush brings up Al-Qaeda, I lean in, watching his lips closely to make sure I catch every single word. "They are a group of Islamic extremists who are rejected by Muslim leaders," he says.

Suddenly, I want to drag Mom out of bed and make her listen. Even if Sam's grandparents are Muslim, and I guess even if Sam decides he wants to be one, they're not all terrorists. They're not the enemy.

I grab a cushion and pull it to my chest. The people on TV clap and stand after every few sentences. He's firing up the crowd. And me, too. My heart and head swell with pride, especially when he says, "You are either with us, or you are with the terrorists."

I can't help myself. I yell, "Yes, exactly!" And it's the same here. The way I see it, my friends are either with me and Sam or with Bobby. There's no middle ground. Bobby is terrorizing Sam, and it needs to stop.

I feel like I did that night at the candle vigil, surrounded by people who make me feel good instead of bad. I wish more than anything, at that moment, that I was old enough to enlist. When he says, "The hour is coming when the military will be called to act," I almost jump in the air. I wish I could be one of the people who makes our country proud and safe. I wonder if Sam or even Kirk feel the same way. Or is Kirk afraid of dying like his Dad? Isn't it better to die a hero than to be alive simply because you were too scared to stand up and fight for what's right?

I'm lost in my own head until I hear the president say that tons of FBI agents are working on the case and if they ask for our help, we should give it. Well, Mr. Madina did try to help and then they took him. The FBI definitely got this wrong—even if it's just this one time.

Dad's cheeks are red and he looks choked up when President Bush ends his speech with the hope that God will watch over the United States of America, but all the patriotism I felt a few minutes ago is now gone.

"That was quite a speech." Dad puts his hand on my shoulder and squeezes.

I nod and stand, feeling less sure of everything than ever.

"I talked to your mom. There's no reason for you to be missing school, but you have to promise you're going to let this thing with Bobby go and stop your fighting."

I can't help but roll my eyes. "Bobby starts it. Am I supposed to just walk away from him?" Then I remember the night Dad walked away from Mr. Brinkmann at Mullins Park. Of course he wants me to walk away. He doesn't want me to stand up to the enemy, as the president just said.

"If it means you staying out of trouble, then, yes. Do you really think you can change Bobby by physically fighting him?"

Yes, I do. Bobby needs to stop being so ignorant. Even if he doesn't change, he can't get away with being a punk. But I don't tell Dad any of this. He doesn't seem to want to hear my real thoughts.

"I mean it. You either promise to stay away from him or you stay home."

"Fine." I walk toward my room. "I won't start anything with him." It's not a lie because I only promised not pick a fight with Bobby. But I never promised I wouldn't finish one.

CHAPTER 15
SEPTEMBER 21, 2001
FRIDAY

....

I look at the board for today's journal question, bracing myself for a three-paragraph narrative on what I hope to find at the end of the rainbow or some other completely ridiculous prompt. Instead, it reads:

Today is: September 21
International Day of Peace
Established by the United Nations in 1981

I'm happy to be spared another dumb question, because I can't afford any more incompletes or zeros on these make-believe scenarios.

Bobby and Rigo walk in together just as the bell rings. Matt sees me and hangs back from them. I nod, but he looks away.

Bobby goes out of his way to pass my desk, then gets up in my face and says, "Boo! How'd that meet go? Oh, wait, you didn't get to run, did you? Mommy came and took you home." He laughs.

I don't move an inch, but it takes everything in me not to deck him again. I clench the edge of my desk, but it's no use. Anger rips through me and I jump up.

Mrs. Cruz steps between us. "Move away, Bobby, or you'll find yourself suspended."

He smirks at me, then takes a seat across the room.

The blood's raging in my veins as Mrs. Cruz motions me back into my seat.

I peel my eyes away from Bobby when Katie and some girl I've never seen before come on the TV screen for announcements. The new girl is boring; so is Katie. I guess I never realized how funny Aamber is. I wish she and Sam would come back to school.

When announcements are over, Mrs. Cruz stands. "As you know, our annual Peace Rally was planned for next week. I know you all have been working hard on it, but after everything that's happened lately, the administration thinks it might be a good idea to cancel it. I told them I thought that was the worst thing they could do, especially now. It took some prodding, but we're still on."

A couple of kids groan. I can't help but do the same. Who can think about peace right now?

Mrs. Cruz taps the board. "We'll work on that next week. Today, we're going to talk about treaties."

More groans. Then Katie opens the door and finds her seat.

Mrs. Cruz continues, "I know it might not sound interesting, but let me tell you why it's important." She writes WWII on the board. "Does anyone know why World War II started?"

Katie's hand shoots up and she doesn't wait to be called on: "Because of Hitler."

Mrs. Cruz writes Hitler on the board. "Yep, that's part of it, but go deeper."

I would have said the same thing and I'm not sure what else could have started it.

"Come on. Take a guess." She paces each aisle. "How do you think Hitler got control? Or why?" She taps my desk. "Jake?"

I'm embarrassed because as much as I love history, I don't know the answer. Sam and I talk about battles all the time, but other than the Revolutionary War or the Civil War, I'm not sure why any other wars were started.

She doesn't leave my side and it's obvious she wants an answer, so I shrug. "How does anyone get control? I guess power, and you only get power when someone else lets you. The Germans liked Hitler for some reason."

"Good." She dashes for the front of the room and writes WEAK in big letters. "Anyone know why Germany was weak?"

When no one else answers after a few seconds, she says, "If anyone ever asks you why World War II began, you can always say it is because of the treaty that ended World War I."

I'm confused, but I'm curious.

"The details about these two wars are not what I want to focus on today, but I'll tell you this. The allied powers, after they won the First World War, were in no mood to be charitable to the losers. In the Treaty of Versailles, Germany was crippled financially, socially, and physically, but perhaps more importantly, they were forced to take full blame for the start of the war and to sign the treaty even though they felt it was unfair. Resentment penetrated deeply throughout the German citizens. This is what paved the way for such an influential man like Hitler to come in and grab power so easily. The Germans were depressed and Hitler promised them the world, giving them one very important thing at a time they needed it most." She looks around at each of us. "Anyone know what it was?"

Katie answers again. "Hope?"

"Right. Great job." Mrs. Cruz writes that on the board and it reminds me for a second about what Father O'Reilley said during Mass last week—that fear must be replaced by hope.

"Let's take this one step further." Mrs. Cruz switches from a blue to a green marker and writes WHY STUDY HISTORY? on the board. "Last week, when I asked you to journal about this, some of you had typical free-write answers, but one of you wrote a perfect, if too-short, answer."

How can an answer be too short if it's perfect? The classroom is silent.

"Jake, tell us what you wrote."

Me? "Uh, just that if we know something didn't work in the past, don't let it happen again. Or, if something worked great, stick with that."

"Exactly." She sits on top of her desk. "Today is the international day for peace and the reason I wanted to talk about treaties is because if we learn nothing else from the outbreak of World War II, remember that winning isn't always the final objective. It's what we do after we win that determines the future. We need to learn from the past."

For homework, Mrs. Cruz tells us to compare the

treaties that ended World War I and World War II. Did historians learn anything from the first one that changed the terms of the second?

I'm actually curious to get home and look this up, because after the Japanese bombed Pearl Harbor and we kicked their butt, I figured our treaty nailed them. But, if what Mrs. Cruz is suggesting is true, and there's been no WWIII, maybe we went easy on them. I really want to find out.

....

Mom and Dad both pick me up from practice in the pouring rain, and I can't help but think they're together because they expect that I got into a fight with Bobby again. When Coach smiles and waves to them, I swear Mom's shoulders relax.

We make a stop at the grocery store on the way home. Dad grabs the umbrella and the three of us go inside. I haven't been to the store since the day of the attacks, but just like that time—yet unlike any other time I've ever been—everyone's overly friendly. The aisles are filled with people talking—shopping carts pushed to the side. It's eerie in its own way.

Dad and I head for the meat section. On our way back up front, we pass Mom. She's standing between an aisle and a cashier. She tries to stop mid-sentence when she sees me, but the lady next to her is shaking her head and saying, "Gosh, who would have ever guessed? They seemed like such nice people."

It's like someone's wrapped their hands around my throat. I can't breathe. She's obviously spreading the news about Mr. Madina and the FBI. She's a traitor. Not just to the Madina's, but to me. How could she talk about Sam's family like that, without knowing the whole story?

My stomach's pushing in on itself and I'm gonna be sick.

Mom looks at the floor.

Suddenly I scream, "You're a liar! He didn't do anything." I sprint out of the store, into the pouring rain. I hate her. Dad, too. I can't live with them anymore.

They pull up beside me as I enter our neighborhood, but I don't even look at them. I pass Sam's. That's where I need to be—with normal people. With my friend. Not stuck at home with parents who have lost their minds.

When I reach our house, I wait for my parents to park and then unlock the door. Mom tries to hug me, but I pull away. I head to my room—water dripping on the floor all the way.

I hear Mom cry as she and Dad argue in their bedroom with the door closed. I grab my gym bag and stuff clothes in. Just before zipping it, I reach for Grandpa's medal, wishing more than anything he was here right now. He'd understand me needing to stick up for my friend—that you never leave a man behind.

I open my window, sling my gym bag over my shoulder, and escape out into the rain.

....

I ring the bell over and over. It takes a while, but finally Aamber opens the door. "Hey," she says.

Sam comes up behind her, his hair messed up and sweat dripping down the sides of his face. It seems like weeks since we've hung out and it's good to see him.

I leave my wet shoes on the front porch and come inside. "Can I stay here? My mom's out of control. I don't even know how I could possibly be related to her. And my dad just sits there and let's her act crazy. He lets her sit in her room and stare at walls. He—" I feel bad for ranting because I know Sam and Aamber have it way worse than me right now. "Never mind. Can I just stay for a while?"

Sam takes my bag from me and tosses it on the couch. "Sure."

"Has your dad called yet?"

He shakes his head. "I've called the police station at least thirty times. They won't tell me anything. I don't even know who else to ask."

I was nervous coming over here because I wasn't sure how Sam would be. He's been so hot and cold the last few times I've seen him, but this is the Sam I know. My best friend. "Well, I have an idea. I'm going to ask my uncle to help us find your dad. Even if he doesn't know anything, I'm sure he knows someone who can find out more information."

A slow smile stretches across Sam's face. "That's a great idea. Seriously, Jake. Thanks."

"He's doing a fundraiser at Mullins Park tomorrow. We can meet him there at ten."

Sam slaps my back and it's the first time I've seen him happy in a while.

Aamber waves us into the garage. "If you're going to stay, you can help us look for the phone number of my dad's lawyer. Dad stores everything out here."

Sam takes a box down from the shelf and lifts the lid. I watch him. I can't help but wonder why Mr. Madina would have needed a lawyer before—or now—but I quickly put the thought out of my mind when I hear a car door slam outside the garage.

I jump and whisper, "I, uh, didn't tell my parents I left. It's probably them."

Aamber holds her arm out. "Stay here."

The doorbell rings.

She paces in the kitchen and motions for me to close

the door all the way, but I want to hear. Sam swings the front door wide open.

Dad sets his umbrella down, then steps inside. "I'm sorry to barge in." He's out of breath and wrings his hands together. "Is Jake here? Have you seen him?" My bag's on the couch in the living room. *Don't let him see it. Please don't see it.*

He scans the room, then sighs so deep I can hear it from my hideout.

Sam says, "Nope. He's not here."

"Right. Are you sure he's not in your room or something?"

Sam shakes his head.

The rain picks up and I have to strain harder to hear.

Dad says, "It's just that we're really worried." He looks around again. "Can you at least give him a message?"

Sam nods.

"Tell him everything's going to be fine. He should just come home."

Sam says coolly, "I'm glad everything's going to be fine for you and your family. I'll be sure to tell him."

"I didn't mean it like that. Things are going to turn around for you all, too. But right now, both of us are missing someone we love."

"Yeah, but my dad didn't leave by choice."

Dad steps onto the porch and I see him trip on a

shoe—my shoe. I hold my breath and wait for it. He pokes his head back in and says extra loud. "Please tell Jake to call home."

Sam closes the door.

I should've stood up to Dad instead of making Sam lie for me, but I need more time to figure everything out. I open the door from the garage and take a seat in the kitchen. "Sorry about that."

Sam says, "He knows you're here, but you should call him anyway. At least he came looking for you."

I don't answer because I'm still mad at Dad for not standing up to Mom or Mr. Brinkmann.

Aamber grabs the garage door handle. "Come on, let's finish looking. Maybe we'll find Dad's papers out here, too. I've looked everywhere in the house and it's like they've disappeared or something."

My head jerks toward Sam. "Papers?"

His face goes red as he turns from me and quickly heads into the garage.

I wait in the kitchen for Aamber to explain.

She says, "Yeah. I mean, if the FBI took him because there's a problem with his immigration papers, maybe if we find the copy Dad made of them, they'll see it was a mistake. He keeps extras of everything."

A problem with his papers? What do they even mean by *papers*? Why didn't Sam tell me this before?

Aamber snaps her fingers in front of my eyes. "Earth to Jake. What's the matter?"

"What do you mean your dad's papers?"

"Come on. That's why the FBI took him. They claim there's a problem with them. Like they're not legit or something."

I shake my head, over and over, hoping the motion will juggle the thoughts into the right places. Places where everything will make sense again. "I had no clue. Aren't immigration papers for someone who isn't a citizen?"

"Not necessarily, but in my dad's case, he got a green card when he and my mom got married. He's been studying to be a citizen on and off for years." She sighs. "Honestly, how did you *not* know this?"

Sam. I didn't know because Sam never told me. I hear him banging around in the garage. Did he keep it from me on purpose?

Aamber pulls me toward the garage. "It's all a scam, though. They think my dad's connected because Atta had Dad's business card. I think they're just using the papers as an excuse to question him more."

Sam mumbles, "Or to keep him from running."

The blood bolts through my veins. "But why would he run? He didn't do anything, right?"

Sam scowls at me. "Wow. That's like the fourth time

you've asked me that. Maybe you don't believe he's innocent, either. It's pretty obvious your mom and dad don't."

He hands me a flashlight even though the garage light's on. "You going to help us or not?" The storm's kicking outside and none of us want to be stuck in the dark if the power goes out.

I'm so confused. What am I actually helping them with? Aamber's big brown eyes lock with mine. I've known the Madinas practically my whole life, but now I feel as if I don't know them at all. I shake the feeling off, though. Sam's my friend.

We pick through boxes of stuff piled against the wall. I get on my hands and knees to grab one that's shoved under a tall, skinny table. Something to my right shines. I crawl under the table and pull out a small box. The tiny tiles glued on the top form a picture. It looks like a C or maybe a part of a moon. I open it; there's a book called *Al-Qur'an*. I've seen that word before. I flip though the book, but it's not in English and for a second the hairs on my arms stand, so I stick it back in the box.

The thunder grumbles again. Lightning cracks and I jump, dropping the flashlight. The beam of light catches the glass of a picture frame with a yellow background. It looks like a tree. I slide it out. Underneath it reads: 99 NAMES OF ALLAH and all of them are listed. Allah.

I've heard that, too. It was in the newspaper in an article about Atta.

I push it away. *Breathe. Just breathe.* But I can't. Mr. Madina was piling this stuff up just last week. Maybe he *is* hiding something. *No. No! Dumb.* I flip the picture to face the wall and shove it behind a box.

Sam squats next to me. "You look kind of pale. Are you okay?"

My head thumps into the underside of the table "Yeah." I shake off my jitters. "I didn't see anything with a phone number or any law papers, though."

"Me either," Aamber says.

Sam flips off his flashlight. "This was a stupid idea. I'm going to check on Mom, then go to bed." He pushes his way past boxes and into the house.

Lightning cracks again and we all scramble into the house. Inside I won't have to think about the stuff that's piled out there.

Aamber gives me a hug. I don't expect it and my arms hang by my side. "Thanks for your help," she says.

"Thanks for hiding me," is all I can say in return.

She grabs her pillow and heads into her Mom's room.

Sam's already in his bed when I open the door. He asks me again. "You sure you're okay?"

"Why do you keep asking me that?"

He points to a sleeping bag rolled up near the closet.

"Just checking." He doesn't say anything else as he turns over.

I spread the sleeping bag on the floor. All I want is to sleep and forget about all the stuff in the garage or that my best friend's keeping secrets from me. I turn out the light. The thunder and lightning won't quit. I pull the sleeping bag tighter as the storm rages like the thoughts in my head. Sam's dad's not even a citizen. Is something really wrong with his papers? Allah. *Al-Qur'an*. Mr. Madina has a lawyer? *Just go to sleep.* But I feel off. I reach into my pocket and pull out Grandpa's medal, clutching it in my fist as I close my eyes and pray for sleep.

CHAPTER 16
SEPTEMBER 22, 2001
SATURDAY

....

Mrs. Madina set a steaming bowl of spaghetti on the table. If it were my house, I'd lunge for it, but I'm at Sam's, so I wait for the bowl to be passed around.

The doorbell rings. Mr. Madina gets up to answer it and I suddenly notice the extra place set at the table. He opens the door and says something in another language.

Mohamed Atta walks in. I recognize him from the news. He says the exact same thing back to Mr. Madina, followed by, "I've brought you a gift."

The book. It's the book from the garage. I look at Sam and yell, "You know Atta?"

I bolt upright. I'm drenched in sweat. I hold my chest and force myself to suck in air. It's still pouring outside. The nightmare seemed so real. They knew Atta. In my dream, they knew him. I look at Sam. He's asleep.

I jerk my head back and forth, scouring the dream from my brain. *It's not real.* The trees gush in the wind outside and shadows float across the walls. *So Sam's Muslim like the terrorists. And his garage is filled with boxes of Muslim stuff. They're storing it away. Or hiding it? Because Mr. Madina's not even a US citizen. And the FBI knows it. All of it.*

Out. I have to get out now. I tear through the house and bolt out the front door. Running. Barefooted. Sprinting. Fast.

I run into the Wilkeys' yard. Something grunts in the darkness. It's coming from the porch. I freeze. My head says run but my feet won't move. The lightning strikes and, for a split second, the sky's like daylight. And there's his face. It's covered with red patches. Swollen. The thunder cracks. I hear shuffling. He's getting closer. I jump and stifle a scream. *Get out of here now.* I take off again—into the black, rainy night.

....

When I sit up on the lounge chair on our back porch, the sun's out in full force.

"Morning." Dad's sipping coffee in the chair next to me.

I have nothing to say to him. I tug at my wet shirt to pry it off my skin.

Everything's running together. I didn't get attacked by Mr. Wilkey, though he was definitely coming for me. I wasn't struck by lightning. Nothing happened to me at Sam's. But, Sam. Aamber. Mr. Madina. It all comes back as my eyes adjust to the light: the garage, the box, the picture.

My eyes burn. I squish them closed, trying to put everything together. Why would I ever think that the Madinas are bad? It was just dark and I wasn't expecting to see that stuff. And Mom's voice kept popping in my head.

I want to ask Dad if he knew Mr. Madina wasn't really a citizen, but I don't want to give him and Mom more ammo against Sam's family in case it's news to them. My insides feel flipped, though, and I wish I could talk about it to someone.

Dad shakes me. "Are you okay?" His eyebrows wrinkle. "You've worried me these last few days."

"I've worried *you?*" I pull away from his grip. "Everyone else is acting crazy around here, and you're worried about *me?*"

"You ran away, Jake. You've never done that before. And you're picking fights at school."

I jump up. "There you go again. I am *not* picking fights. Bobby's picking fights."

He runs his hands through his hair. "Regardless, you're fighting. It's not like you."

"Yeah, well maybe this is the new me." I storm toward the house.

"Hold it, right there." He stands. "You will not talk to me like that. You need to take ownership of what you've been doing lately. Until you do, you're grounded."

"What? But tomorrow's the Dolphin game."

"Sorry. You're not going."

"You can't be serious! It's my birthday present. You can't just take it back!"

"You've left us no choice."

There's a pounding in my ears. My chest grows hot and I want to . . . want to . . . I don't know. My thoughts are suddenly fuzzy.

"As for your mom," Dad closes his eyes and sighs. "I know she's not herself. I'm doing the best I can, but give me a break. There's a lot you don't know."

"I'm sick of hearing you all say that. Either tell me what I need to know, or stop using it as an excuse for how she's behaving." I push past him, needing the quiet of my room. I reach in my pocket for Grandpa's medal but it's not there. I drop back onto the patio chair.

Dad rushes to my side. "What's the matter? You're white as a ghost."

I swallow. "Nothing." I grip the side of the chair and force myself to take a giant breath. "I left my stuff at Sam's. Can I at least go get it before you ground me?"

He inspects my eyes and touches my cheek. "Are you sure that's all?"

I nod.

"I'll drive you over there after breakfast, but you're coming right home."

So the prison sentence can begin.

....

Dad pulls into Sam's driveway. "You go ahead. I'll wait here."

Aamber answers the door. "Hey."

"Thanks again for hiding me out last night."

"No problem. I was surprised when I saw that you left before we got up and didn't take your stuff, though."

I shove my hands in my pockets. "Yeah, I needed to get a run in this morning." My stomach sinks at the lie, but I can't fess up that I freaked out in the middle of the night. "Is Sam around?"

"No, but come in."

It's strange to think that only a week ago we were trying to out-prank each other. I step inside. "Thanks. So, where is he?"

She hesitates. "He went to Mullins Park. I thought you were meeting him there."

"Oh no, I forgot." I'm so stupid. I totally forgot about talking to Uncle Hugh. I look at the clock. "I can still meet him there." I rush to Sam's room to get my things. I can't come out empty-handed or Dad will think I was lying about this, too, but I need to hurry and find a way to meet Sam.

I check for the medal in my bag and on the floor. I shake out the sleeping bag, then look under Sam's bed, in his bed, and in the closet. But the medal is gone. I close my eyes and think. I definitely had it in my grip when I fell asleep. I search more.

I throw open the bedroom door and yell for Aamber.

"Shhh, you're going to wake my mom."

The front door closes and Sam makes his way down the hallway. "What are you doing here?"

"Do you have the medal? My grandpa's medal? It's gone. It was here last night."

Aamber shakes her head.

Mrs. Madina calls and Aamber goes to her.

I turn to Sam. "Come on, Sam. Do you have it? Please, you know how important it is to me."

"It's always about *you*."

"Look, I'm sorry about this morning. I'm going to help you find your dad. I'll talk to Uncle Hugh. I promise. Can't you just help me find the medal?"

Sam shoots me a nasty look. "You sure you still want to help *us*?"

"What? Of course I do. I told you last night I would. I'm sorry I blanked out this morning."

"That's not all you said last night."

"What are you talking about?"

He folds his arms over his chest. "I saw the way you looked when you were poking through the boxes. You were scared. Then you yelled something about us knowing Atta in your sleep and took off in the middle of the night in a freaking storm. You're as bad as your parents."

Did I yell that out loud? I wipe my sweaty hands on my pants. "You're wrong. I was just surprised by the things in the garage because I read about some stuff in the newspaper. They found a *Qur'an* in Atta's car. And then you had one here. I'd never seen anything like it before. It just surprised me, that's all." I take a breath. "Besides, I can't help what I dream. I never thought anything bad."

It's a lie, of course. I did. But only for a few minutes. And I hate myself for it. "How come you never told me your Dad's not a US citizen?"

Sam's eyes narrow and if they could shoot darts they would. "I don't have to tell you everything. Or anything. Just leave."

"Come on, Sam."

"Get out, now!"

Sam points to the door. I grab my bag and storm out of his room.

Aamber stops me in the living room. "What's up with you two?"

"I'm sure he'll tell you all about it, but believe me, it's not true. I gotta go. My dad's waiting." But I need to find that medal before Dad comes looking for me. "Um, I dropped something in your garage so I'll go out that way, okay?"

I head to the garage and out the side door. I close my eyes. *Think.* It must've been in my hand when I left last night. And I ran. To the Wilkeys'. *Oh no!*

I slip around the side of Sam's house and over to the Wilkeys'. From the sidewalk, I strain my neck to look at where I stood last night when Mr. Wilkey came after me. There's nothing shiny in the yard, but I can't see all that well from here. I dart to the middle of the grass. I look in the flower bed, the bushes, and even get close enough to look on the porch. But the medal's gone. Just like my breath.

I take short gasps, but it doesn't help. My body's weak . . . but heavy. I look toward Mr. Wilkey's window. I bet he has it. He has to.

....

I throw my bag on the kitchen floor and Mom jumps out of her daze as she stands over the sink.

The anger from the night before in the grocery store and from my fight with Sam has me pumped. I hate myself for doubting Mr. Madina, but it was Mom's voice in my head that made me have that nightmare. It's all her fault. She should know what she's doing to me. "So, Mrs. Madina hasn't gotten out of bed since Tuesday. Sam won't talk to me because he knows what you think of them, and Aamber's just trying to hold everyone together over there."

Mom's back's facing me but her shoulders are moving up and down with each deep breath. After a few seconds, she turns around. "Why are you doing this to us? You're doing this on purpose, aren't you?"

"No, *you're* doing this. Why are you being so mean to them?" I'm at the sink and begging. "Can't you help them? Please! Ground me for life. But please, help them!

You have to ask Uncle Hugh to try to find something out. He has connections."

Mom's still breathing hard as she grips the counter.

I calm down and plead with her. "How can you say no? Sam and Aamber don't even know where their dad is. You help the Wilkeys, but never think of helping Mrs. Madina who's supposed to be your friend. I don't understand!"

Mom brings the dishtowel to her face and closes her eyes. She's whiter than the cabinets.

"I can't," is all she says.

"You mean, you won't."

She yells, "You don't know what you're talking about Jake! You can't put yourself out there like that. Just stick to home. It's the only way to keep yourself from getting hurt."

"I'm not gonna stick to home. I can't. I need to help my friends, even if you won't."

She shakes her head quick and fast, over and over. "No, I won't let you. You hear me? Stop it, Jake!" Mom slams a plate on the counter, smashing it to pieces.

Suddenly Dad and Grandma are in the kitchen with us. I didn't even realize Grandma had come over. She grabs me and pulls me close.

Dad puts his arms around Mom. "Calm down," he whispers.

Mom sobs and wriggles free of him. "I will *not* calm down. I won't go through this again. If Jake gets involved he's going to get hurt and it won't just be by Bobby Brinkmann."

Grandma reaches for Mom's hand without letting go of me, drawing us all together. "It's okay."

"No, it's not!" She swats Grandma away and points at me. "You want to save the world just like Grandpa and look where it got him." Mom's gasping so much I think she might not be able to get air in. Dad forces her into a chair.

I slowly sit next to her. I've never seen her like this and as mad as I am, I can't help but think she's about to lose it for good.

"Look," Dad's arms are wrapped around Mom, "maybe it's time to tell Jake about your dad's death. He's right. We can't expect him to understand if we don't explain it to him. He's old enough now to hear the truth."

Mom's whole body shakes and the tears stream down her cheeks. She buries her face in her hands and stays like that for a long time, until she runs out of tears, or energy, or both. When she finally looks up, her eyes are puffed like cotton balls. I get up and hug her, because I want her to calm down. I don't want her to go back to the staring place.

Dad looks at her and nods in my direction.

"I don't know. It's just so . . . ugly." After a minute she says, "Well, you know he died—"

I sit back down. "In the war, I know." I want her to get to the part I've never heard before.

"What?" Mom clears her throat. "No, he was never in a war."

Of course he was. I look at Dad. Then I look at Grandma. "But you said he died overseas. You always talk about him in the service, and he got a medal."

There's suddenly a loud sigh from everyone in the room. Grandma takes my hand. "Oh, honey. You have it wrong."

Mom shakes her head. "He wasn't a soldier. He was an ambassador for the United States."

"What? That makes no sense."

Grandma says, "It's true."

"Why would you all let me think he—"

Dad puts his hand up. "Hang on, Champ. No one ever said he was in the military. I guess I can see how you'd think that, and I guess we never talked about the specifics much, but listen. Your mom will explain."

I'm steaming mad. At them, but at myself, too, for being such a sucker.

"My dad," she pauses, "was stationed in the Middle East for a long time. That might be why you heard us say he was in the service. For a while, Grandma lived with him, too, but once I was born, he thought it was too dangerous for us to be there, so Grandma and I moved back to the states. Every time he'd come home, I'd beg him to stay with us." Tears gush from Mom's eyes again.

Grandma wipes her cheeks, too.

Mom sniffles and says, "I begged him to find a new job. One where he could be home, or at least be in the country. He finally agreed that when I got to middle school he would, but he felt he had to finish out his term because what he was doing over there was important, too." Mom takes another sip of water before continuing. "He was set to come home in April, just in time for my thirteenth birthday. I decided that instead of a birthday party, I wanted to have a welcome home party. So Grandma and I made the invitations, cleaned and decorated the house, and planned the meal. The night before he was supposed to leave Sudan, he went to another embassy for a dinner party. It was a goodbye party for him and a welcome party for the man who was taking his place."

My heart squeezes itself so hard I feel like a tank's parked on my chest. I swallow the lump in my throat.

Mom slides her water glass back and forth across the table. "Well, some guys stormed in with masks on. They took Grandpa and some others hostage. They were part of a terrorist group called Black September. Their leader called President Nixon and demanded that we release their prisoners or else they'd kill all the hostages. Nixon refused. It was too big of a risk and no guarantee the terrorists would release the hostages anyway. Or maybe he was calling their bluff, as some reports say. Regardless, those monsters followed through on their threat. Only they didn't kill all of the hostages. Just three."

Grandma's eyes are closed, but the tears still escape them.

Dad turns to me and I look away. The bottom of my stomach's twisted with hatred and anger for what I'm hearing. We sit there for a long time.

Finally, I say, "So the Black September group, were they Muslims?"

Grandma shakes her head. "They claimed to be secular, but they were Arabs."

Mom's words are muffled from her crying. "It's like we're not even safe in our own country anymore. They're coming for us here."

"They?" I say. "It could have been anybody with a freak cause, not just an Arab Muslim."

She's quiet for a second, then nods. "Exactly."

A nod. She agrees.

"So, you think if we hang a flag, or just be ourselves, we'll be targeted?"

"We just don't need to get involved either way," Mom says.

"Please Mom," I beg, standing in front of her, "the Madinas aren't part of that Black September group. They aren't the enemy. They need us. We're not gonna get attacked just by asking Uncle Hugh or anyone else if they can find out where Mr. Madina is. The Madinas aren't terrorists"

She shakes her head. "I'm sorry. I just can't."

"Have you always hated them? I mean, for being Muslim?" I ask.

"Hate's a strong word, so no. When you first met Sam, it was hard. His mom was so nice at the park that day, but I admit I tried hard to avoid getting together with them after that. Then I kept running in to her everywhere and you and Sam were like magnets. It took everything in me to eventually be friends with her, but I did—for you. I don't mean to push them away, but until we're sure they're clear, until the FBI can prove it, how can we trust them?"

"Because we know them."

She stands. "I'm sorry, but I can't help them. Please stop asking me." She heads to her room and Grandma follows.

Dad reaches for me, but I pull away. I'm furious. All this time I had it wrong. Grandpa wasn't a soldier. Or a hero. He never even fought in any war. How could I have been so dumb? Soldiers are brave. They enlist knowing they might get killed, but Grandpa didn't even carry a weapon. So why would those people murder him? Why doesn't anything make sense anymore?

CHAPTER 17

....

Dad wakes me. "Come on, Champ. Time for church."

I wish he'd stop calling me that, like I'm a little kid. "I have a headache and I barely slept." This isn't a lie—I was up most of the night.

Grandma comes in from the hall. "Why don't you let him sleep today?"

"No, he's grounded, and he's going to do what we say."

She puts her hand on Dad's arm. "I don't doubt he has a headache after all the information he's been given. Remember, everyone deals with things in their own way and in their own time."

Grandma has this magical way of talking sometimes. I think she could have sweet talked those Black September guys out of killing Grandpa if she'd been there. I prop myself up on one arm, but I already know he's about to give in.

He throws his hands in the air. "Fine, but you're not to go anywhere. And when I get back, you're going to go to the Wilkeys' to cut the grass."

I roll over and close my eyes, waiting for them both to leave.

....

Grandma and Dad left for church. Mom's locked up in her room again and, if I'm fast, I can be to Sam's and back in twenty minutes. I know we left things on bad terms, but I can't stand fighting with him and I need to tell him about Grandpa. I need him to help me figure everything out.

....

Sam's head bobs up and down over the top of his backyard fence. I open the gate and see him cleaning the pool.

"Hey," I say.

He keeps skimming, ignoring me.

So I get right next to him and say, "What's up?"

"What's up?" He snorts. "Are you serious?"

"Sorry. I've never had to think about what to say to you before."

"Look, I'm busy."

"I'm really sorry about not meeting you yesterday. And for the stupid nightmare I had. None of it means anything. I want you to know that I'm going to call Uncle Hugh today."

Sam weaves the skimmer around trying to rescue a frog. "If you really wanted to talk to your uncle, I'm sure you'd have called him by now."

It's true that Mom's big reveal threw me for a loop and I forgot about Uncle Hugh, but it wasn't on purpose. "I'm going to call him as soon as I get home. I am. Promise."

He ignores me again.

"Will you please let me help? There's got to be more we can do besides Uncle Hugh."

"What are you gonna do? Strap on a Navy Seal outfit and storm the prison? We're not seven anymore. This isn't pretend."

"I know it's not pretend. I'm not stupid."

He glances at me for just a second. Then he sucks in a deep breath and looks at the sky. "I don't even know if Dad's alive."

Both his words and sudden change in attitude jolt me. "Look, they should never have taken him. He didn't do anything wrong—I'm sure of it. And they're not gonna kill him." I say this to make him feel better, but Sam clearly reads this the wrong way.

"Yeah? And why is that? Because they're American cops and they don't do that stuff? Taking an innocent man is just as bad as committing terrorist acts."

My eyes scan his face. He can't be serious. There's no way he already forgot what we saw on TV that morning because those things have stuck in my mind like superglue. Taking his dad in and blowing people up are definitely not the same thing.

Sam goes back to skimming.

I hate this. "Look, I just want to help."

He finally catches the frog and sets it down on the deck. "I know, but there's nothing you can do."

I nudge the frog away from the pool with my foot. Sam's right. All I can do is call Uncle Hugh when I get home. I was hoping this conversation would go better and that Sam would go with me to Mr. Wilkey's or at least help me figure out about the medal. I wish we *were* seven again and we could plan some epic scheme to get the medal back—together. "Mr. Wilkey has my grandpa's medal, by the way."

Sam's eyes grow wide. "How'd that happen?"

"I must've dropped it in his yard on Friday when I . . ." The frog jumps over my foot and heads back for the pool.

Sam finishes for me. "When you took off from my house in the middle of the night?"

I nod. "I'm really, really sorry."

"Whatever. I don't care anymore."

I don't get it. I don't get him. Forget the medal and Uncle Hugh. I need to find something to talk to him about—something he likes, just to fix things between us. "Do you like going to the mosque?"

He nods but doesn't look at me. "It's not about some crazy Jihad like people are saying. Islam is actually all about peace."

I have no idea what Jihad means and I've never really heard anything about Muslims before the last few weeks. Maybe a lot people haven't either and that's why everyone's so freaked out after the attacks.

Sam shakes his head. "You don't believe me, do you?"

On my knees, I wrestle the frog, who's determined to jump back into the pool, and don't answer right away.

"Geez, you can't even answer my question. You *are* just like your parents."

I throw my hands up. "I was just about to explain why I *do* believe you, even without knowing anything about it, but you didn't give me a chance."

"Just forget it, Jake. I don't want to hear what you think, anyway."

I want to run over and shake him till the old Sam

comes back. "Really? Because I'll tell you this. You say Islam isn't bad, but ever since you've been going to that mosque, you're different. You're mean, and you only think about yourself. So you can tell me they're not bad and they're all about peace, but if it's true, then why are you acting like such a jerk? Maybe they *are* all bad. Every one of them!" I have no idea where the words came from, or even if I believe them, but I can't take them back now that they're out in the open.

Just then I spot Aamber standing in the doorway holding three glasses of lemonade. It's obvious she saw me go off on Sam. Her eyes squint and she shakes her head at me. "You should go home, Jake."

"Leave us alone," I say.

She walks over to Sam and they both stare me down.

Forget the frog. If he wants to be sucked up by the pool vacuum, let him. I glance at Sam one last time, remembering when he and I conquered ants in the sand-box and took over enemy territories up and down our street. It doesn't seem that long ago, really. I know Sam and I are way too old to play soldiers anymore, but even if we did, I'm not sure we'd still be on the same side.

....

I thought Grandma moved in to keep an eye on Mom,

but Dad took her out for the afternoon and Grandma's still here. Obviously my parents have appointed a new prison guard for me—one who smells like flowers and makes grilled cheese, but one who keeps secrets from me about my grandpa when I never thought she would.

She kisses me on the head. "Lunch, love?"

I shrug.

"We have a busy afternoon. We're going to pop by the Wilkeys' to clean out their shed."

"But I was just there last week. The shed's fine."

"We gotta do what your mom asks. You should learn to pick your battles, Jake."

My whole life is suddenly one prolonged war.

"When we're done there, you need to get crackin' on your homework." She uses the microwave as a mirror as she braids her hair to one side. "You and your mom get your brains from your grandpa. Definitely not from me."

I flinch when she mentions Grandpa; it's not fair for her to bring him up like that, like he's someone I know, because he's like a total stranger to me now. Besides, school is the last thing I care about.

....

The lawnmower's out front again when we pull into the Wilkeys' driveway. Grandma heads up the steps.

"What are you doing?"

She turns to me. "Letting them know we're here. You can start mowing and then we'll clean the shed together. Sound good?" She knocks on the door. Mrs. Wilkey answers, holding the door out for Grandma to come in. If she sees the medal, she'll definitely think I'm irresponsible, and right now, Grandma's the only ally I have left.

I pace out front with the mower on. If the grass could get lower with each pass, it would be bald by now. I slowly make my way around the whole yard, stealing a look at Sam's house every once in a while. There's no sign of him, though, and it's just as well because I have nothing left to say to him.

Just as Grandma comes outside, I finish the last strip. I notice she doesn't have the medal and I can't help but wonder why Mr. Wilkey didn't show her.

"Perfect timing," she says. "The yard looks great. Time to clean out that big cubby." She loops her arm in mine. "Turns out your mom's been picking up prescriptions and running errands for them, too." She slides the shed door open. "Mrs. Wilkey should be back up and running in no time."

That means I can thankfully stop working here soon.

Grandma holds up an ancient-looking radio. "Must be our lucky day." She fiddles with the dial until she hits the oldies station, then grabs my hands and twirls me around to "Burning Love." It's so dorky and I pull away from her, but she keeps on dancing by herself.

When we're almost done organizing, Grandma says, "So, what shall we do next?"

It's obvious what's going on. "Thanks for your help here with the shed, but I don't really need a babysitter all day."

"I know." She sighs. "But you need to think about how you've been handling things, hon. You're such a great kid, but you're not making the best choices lately. You punched Bobby, you've been back-talking your parents, then you ran away. How do you expect your parents to let up on you?"

I can't believe she's taking their side. "I did those things for the right reasons. Bobby deserved it. Mom was telling lies. I didn't do anything wrong! They did. I thought you of all people would understand." I shove past the shed door, storming toward the sidewalk out front.

A cold green Gatorade and another newspaper sit on the bottom porch step. The Wilkeys can keep them. They can keep the medal, too. It doesn't even matter anymore.

....

Grandma asks me to come to dinner, but when I don't answer, she leaves a tray outside my door. There's a plate of chicken and pasta and a newspaper with a note: *Mr. Wilkey wanted you to have this.*

CHAPTER 18
SEPTEMBER 24, 2001
MONDAY

....

Dad said he was taking the week off, but I guess Mom's staying home today, too. I was hoping to fake an illness, but now I'd rather just go to school. Dad drops me off in front of the building and tells me he'll pick me up after practice.

I slip in just after the bell, but Mrs. Cruz is making everyone push all the desks toward the walls of the room so she doesn't even notice. She leaves twelve desks in a wide circle in the middle. Most of us sit in the ones along the wall and wait. Katie and the new girl are already doing the announcements on TV. I scan the room for Aamber. She's here but turns away from me when I catch her eye. I can't help but think of her face yesterday. I didn't mean for her to hear what I said to Sam. I'm not sure I even meant to say it. I don't know where those thoughts came from, but in some way maybe I did mean them, so saying sorry would be a little bit of a lie. I didn't mean to hurt her though. I could apologize for that, but sorry is just a word.

I open my notebook for the daily journal torture. *Would you rather plant a garden of flowers or create a garden of stones?* This assignment is dumb. School is dumb. I scribble, *Flowers are too much work, just like this assignment.* Then I put my head on the desk and tune out the world. I don't even flinch when Bobby pulls out a Xerox copy of a Muslim guy and a pig keychain and makes oinking noises as he holds the two up in a mock kiss. He's not my problem anymore. Nothing is.

Mrs. Cruz snatches the picture from him, crumbling the paper. "See me after class, Bobby. I'd send you to the office now, but you might actually learn something today."

When the announcements finally end, Mrs. Cruz says, "All right class, I have a surprise for you. We're doing a cultural simulation today called The Albatross. Our two volunteers stayed after school last week to help me with this. I expect you'll give them your full attention."

Katie walks in just as Mrs. Cruz is turning on some flashlights and setting them on the floor in the middle of the circle. "Katie, please turn off the lights."

Gina and Ian enter from the hallway. They're dressed in robes—only Ian has shoes on and Gina doesn't. The class laughs and Ian and Gina hiss loudly. Not in a mean way, but we know they want us to stop. They motion for us to come sit around the circle. There aren't enough desks for everyone and when Suzy Lyons takes a seat at a desk, Ian hisses at her. Suzy stands up and Ian motions to the floor. When Suzy takes a seat on the ground, Ian lets out a low hum. It takes a while for us to catch on, but when we finally get it, all of the guys are sitting in desks with shoes on and all of the girls are kneeling on the floor with their shoes off. It feels awkward in a way.

Ian goes and sits on the chair in the center of the room. Gina kneels beside him. After a few seconds, Gina lifts a bowl, takes a pinch of rice, and puts it in Ian's mouth. He grunts and rubs his belly. A few boys laugh and Gina hisses. Some of the girls in the class are scowling.

Gina gets up and goes around the room, dropping rice in the mouths of all the boys.

I hesitate when she gets to me. It's strange that she wants to feed me, especially without a spoon or anything. Finally, I open my mouth and she flicks a few pieces of plain white rice in. It sticks to the top of my mouth.

Most of the girls huff and frown when they get passed by. Then Gina circles again and gives some rice to the girls. Katie flat out refuses to take any. She backs away and presses her lips together. Gina and Ian hiss.

Gina goes back to the middle and there's another long pause. Then she takes a bowl and gives Ian a drink. When he's done, she picks up a tray of paper cups filled with water and gives one to each of the guys. Rebekah Prentess looks like she might explode when Gina passes by her and, when Gina makes a second round giving the girls a turn, Rebekah crosses her arms over her chest and refuses to take a cup at all. Gina hisses but keeps a straight face. Katie snubs the cup, too. When everyone's done, Gina goes back and kneels beside Ian.

Bobby says, "Where's dessert?" Ian and Gina hiss at him and at the people who laugh.

Ian and Gina go around the circle again. They're seriously talking to each other in some grunt language as they inspect the girls' feet. Gina and Ian seem to grunt in agreement for Jenna, and Gina leads her to kneel beside Ian's chair in the center. She goes without any hesitation, but Katie's obviously had enough because she leaves the circle and sits over by the bulletin board, sulking.

Ian and Gina go around the room one last time, doing the same thing they did when they came in. I guess they're saying goodbye. Jenna sits still until Gina takes her by the hand and the three of them leave the room.

We sit in the darkness for another minute. Most of us look around at each other, trying to figure out what the heck that was all about. Katie's still stewing when Mrs. Cruz turns the lights on and Gina, Jenna, and Ian come back into the room.

Mrs. Cruz says, "Katie, want to come back and join us?"

She shakes her head.

"Okay, then. Class, what do you think was happening in the Albatross society?"

Rebekah gives a fake shiver. "It was creepy. They have some weird language and strange ways of doing things."

Katie stands and blurts, "It's a totally male-dominated, outdated society. We should not be promoting that, ya know!"

Mrs. Cruz asks, "Anyone else have an opinion?"

Bobby smacks the desktop. "That's the way it's supposed to be. The girls waiting on the boys and feeding them first." He high-fives Rigo and a couple of guys laugh.

Suzy raises her hand. "I agree with Katie. I mean, how come we had to take our shoes off and sit on the ground?"

Mrs. Cruz says, "Is there any other way that might be interpreted? Think about it. Sometimes things aren't what they seem at first."

The class is silent.

Gina cracks a smile. "Can I tell them, Mrs. Cruz? It's really not what you think at all. See, women in the Albatross society are actually held higher than men in terms of the earth. Women are sorta like one with Mother Nature so they're worthy of walking on the earth barefoot and sitting on the ground. The men aren't." She looks at Bobby and smirks.

Katie bolts upright from her seat.

Bobby yells, "Yeah, well, she had to feed the men and they got to eat first."

"Dude," Ian says, "that's because we can't touch the food and if it's bad or something, we die first. Kinda like a guinea pig. We gotta make sure it's okay before the girls can eat it."

"That's lame." Bobby shoves the desk next to him.

Mrs. Cruz is on her feet fast. "Enough, Bobby. There's a lot to be learned from this exercise. The purpose of this entire thing is to show us how quick we are to judge others and make assumptions without really knowing the facts first."

He shakes his head. "It's dumb. We're fine living just the way we do."

"Are we?" Mrs. Cruz looks at the clock. The bell's about to ring. "I want you to think about this for home-work. List some emotions you felt during the simula-tion, what you felt after you found out about their real culture, and one way you think you can pass this message on to others. We can use some of your ideas when we talk about the peace rally tomorrow."

I've already tried teaching Bobby that there's nothing wrong with Sam or his family, but it didn't work. I think I'll skip this assignment. I look at Aamber and she turns away again. Maybe I'll skip school in general.

....

At practice, I set my stopwatch when coach blows the whistle and don't even bother to pace myself. I can't believe Sam would mess up our team like this. All he thinks about lately is himself. He cares more about his new-found religion than me or the team. I take a longer path than usual to avoid running with the rest of the team. I need to be alone. My feet take over and pick up speed. A tree branch slaps my face and I wish I could chop it off. I turn the corner and my foot catches the edge of a hole. I fall. Hard. My ankle throbs. I grab a rock and chuck it at a tree.

"This sucks. Everything sucks!" I throw another rock and pull myself up using a tree branch but it snaps, sending me to the ground again. My fists pound the dirt. Again. Again. I scream . . . and then I stop. It's hard to breathe in the thick air. I flip onto my back.

Pieces of the sky flicker behind the tree branches—
they're always getting in the way. My ankle pulses to my
heartbeat. I could just stay here. There's no Sam, no
secrets, no Bobby, no crumbled Pentagon or smoking
towers. I could eat berries and dig a hole to sleep in at
night. I could live here and be happy. The Albatross
society isn't real. I don't have to sit in a chair and wear
shoes to keep off the earth. I cover myself with leaves.
The ground underneath is cool. Only my face feels the
hot September air. For years, I imagined my grandpa in
combat, hiding just like this, and it turns out it wasn't
even true. I feel dumb. It'd be easier to dig a trench and
hide out for the rest of my life than deal with all that's
happening.

....

The team's already gone and Coach Rehart's about to
pop a vein when I hobble out of the woods. "I was getting
ready to call 911. What happened to you?"

"I fell."

He examines my ankle. "It doesn't look too bad,
but you should ice it." He helps me to the locker room.
"You're gonna have to rest up if you want to compete
this week."

I nod.

He hands me a bag of ice. "Jake, don't take this the wrong way, but you're a mess. What's happened to you?"

I wish I knew. But I don't, so I can't answer.

"Have you talked to Sam lately?"

"No." Not today anyway.

He puts his foot up on the bench and leans in. "Look, I'm not gonna lecture you. You got benched because shoving Bobby was wrong. But, you're better than that. There are other ways to make a statement without using your fists."

I'm getting sick of hearing that. No one wants to tell me what other ways there are. But I just say, "Okay, Coach."

He sighs loudly. "Try to get Sam to come back to school. He needs to be here. I'm not just saying that for the team's sake." Mr. Rehart tilts his head. "But until he does, you and Kirk will lead the team."

I wished for this when I blew out my candles—the captain band is mine. Now, though, I wish I could take it back. "No, thanks. I don't want it."

We sit on the bench for a long time.

Finally, Coach says, "You can't wobble home on that ankle. Want me to call someone to pick you up?"

"My Dad should be out front."

He looks like he wants to keep talking, but after a few

seconds, he stands and starts walking away. "I'll be in my office if you need me."

"See you, Coach."

....

Grandma's waiting for me when I limp out of the locker room.

I get in the car and she asks, "You okay, hon?"

I'm still mad at her for siding with Mom and Dad, but it's like she doesn't even care that I ran out and left her to finish cleaning the shed alone—like she's already forgiven me or something. I nod. "Yeah."

And that's it. We ride in silence the whole way home. She doesn't try to ask a million questions like Mom would, and that's good because I don't feel like talking, though I do feel bad about being so mean to her yesterday.

CHAPTER 19
SEPTEMBER 25, 2001
TUESDAY

....

My ankle's fine so I can't use it as an excuse to stay home from school, but I need to find a way not to go. I don't want to see anyone. It's all just a big waste of time. I want to stay in bed and disappear.

I tiptoe to the bathroom before anyone wakes up, grab the trashcan, and put it next to my bed. I wet a washcloth and tuck it between my mattress and the wall. Fool proof—as long as it's Dad that comes in and not Mom.

....

A while later, I hear someone in the hallway and grab the washcloth. It's cold and still wet. I turn off the reading lamp that's been warming my forehead for the last ten minutes.

Mom opens my door. "Time to get up."

She'll be tough, but I'm *not* going to school. I moan.

"What's the matter?" She trips on the trashcan as she nears my bed.

I reach for her hand and she touches mine. I moan again.

"You're awful clammy. Let me feel your head." She puts her lips to my forehead. "A little warm. Did you throw up?"

I mumble, "No, but I feel like I'm going to."

She runs her hands through her already messy hair. "Jake, you missed school last week. You're just getting back on track. How long have you been feeling sick?"

I need to play it up more. "Since about four-thirty." I grab my stomach like I might hurl.

"You should have woken me up." She puts her hands on her hips and sighs. "Your dad and I have somewhere to be. I guess, well, Grandma's here, so maybe she can look after you."

I try not to smile victoriously. I don't care who stays with me or even that Mom thinks I need a babysitter. I'm just happy to be staying home. It's crazy to think how she and I ended up like this: each winning small battles, but neither of us ever winning the war.

....

I can't sleep anymore, but I don't really want to get up. The newspaper from Mr. Wilkey is on my nightstand. I glance at the front page. It's the same paper he gave me that first day, the one that has the article about Mr. Stone's death. Then I see a yellow tab sticking out. I open to page 10A. A post-it note reads: *I have something of yours. Come see me.* Does he actually think I'm going to knock on his door after he tried to come after me in the middle of the night? Besides, I don't even want the medal anymore—although for some reason, I can't seem to stop thinking about it.

I look at the paper again. There's also an article circled in red. *It is beneath us to hate on account of religion or ethnicity at any time.* I read the rest. I guess people are picking on Muslims everywhere: in Texas, Illinois, Colorado. And then there was a part about how the US detained hundreds of Japanese-Americans during World War II. How did I not know this? I'd definitely remember if that were in any history books.

As I keep reading, I think about the FBI and Mr. Madina. Maybe there are more people like him that the FBI has taken. Is that what Mr. Wilkey wants to tell me? Or is he warning me to stay away from Sam, like Mom and Dad?

I wrap my blanket around me and peek out of my room. I see Grandma when I get to the kitchen. "I need to use the computer to catch up on some schoolwork. Is that okay?"

She hands me a bowl of soup. "Of course it's okay. You need to keep those grades up."

I take my soup to the living room and log on to the computer. I type in *Japanese detained in America during World War II*. I'm not sure if I'm more shocked or sick by the facts I learn. Thousands of Japanese-Americans were taken away or put in camps by our own government during the war. But isn't this supposed to be the Land of the Free? Maybe they all had problems with their papers, too? Even the kids? I shudder under my blanket, because if things today were like they were back then, Sam and Aamber would be gone, too. My skin pricks.

It's too much to think about, so I click off that site and type in *Meaning of the name Jake*. The first site I click on states that Jake means "Supplanter; held by the heel." I look up the word *supplanter* and it means "to replace." That doesn't even make sense.

I try another site. This one states that Jake is short for Jacob, that it's a Hebrew name, and that in the Bible Jacob wrestled with an angel till daybreak. I wonder who won.

There are so many websites listed with name meanings and I click on at least twelve of them, but none describe a Jake that's me. Then again, I'm not really sure who *me* is anymore.

I hear Grandma's bracelets jingle as she makes her way into the living room. She sits on the couch and pats the empty spot next to her. "Come here, hon. I want to talk to you."

I sit and pull the blanket tighter over my shoulders— even though I'm really sweating underneath. It's hard to stay mad at her.

"I feel bad the way we sprung the news about your grandpa on you, but I want you to know that he loved his job. He liked making a difference in the world."

"But that's what I don't get. What difference did he make?"

"Oh, hon, he was instrumental in reestablishing friendly relations with Sudan after years of hostilities because of the Arab-Israeli War. I can't say he prevented us from going to war for sure, but it's quite possible."

I stare out the window and try to make sense of everything. It's hard to do, though, when, I thought of him one way for so long—a soldier, a fighter. I can't seem to wrap my head around a whole new picture of him. Grandpa might have saved a lot of lives without fighting. But I thought I was just like him. Yet I'm not at all. I think that's what bothers me the most.

I thought Grandpa would have defended his friend, too, but maybe he wouldn't have. I snap out of it and ask, "So he was never a fighter? Ever?"

She stands and opens her arms. I get up and hug her as she says, "Sometimes it takes more courage not to fight. You know, you're brave, just like your grandpa."

After a brief pause, I say, "How come you seem okay with Grandpa's death and Mom isn't?"

"Your grandpa was doing exactly what he was born to do. He had a way of bringing people together and solving problems. It was a gift, and I knew that when I married him. Knowing how much he loved us is what keeps me going. But your mom, she blames herself for asking him to come home. She thinks if she hadn't asked him to, he would have stayed, they never would have had that going away party, and he'd still be alive."

I didn't think of it like that before, but now I can see why Mom would blame herself. I probably would, too.

Grandma smoothes her skirt. "I took her to counseling and we wrote letters to Grandpa so she could feel close to him, but she never fully got over it. It's why she's so strict with you. She wants to protect you from the world and keep you safe. The attacks two weeks ago set her back again. So just give her a bit of a break, okay?"

Part of me wants to, because I do feel bad. She can't change what happened to Grandpa, but she could have helped the Madinas. And she still can.

Grandma kisses the top of my head. "Get back to your schoolwork, hon. You need to keep your brain juiced." She heads into the kitchen.

My head's not into schoolwork. It seems to be stuck on Grandpa's story. But Grandma's wrong. I'm not like him. I'm pretty much alone in my family—just Jake, a stupid supplanter.

....

At dinner, I try to give Mom a break like Grandma asked, so I smile when she talks and Grandma squeezes my hand every once in a while. Dad keeps looking at me, but we still haven't spoken to one another. I notice that he looks tired.

Later, there's a knock at my bedroom door and Grandma enters.

I fold the newspaper and sit up in bed.

"It's time for me to go home," she says, sitting on the edge of my bed.

"But Mom still needs you."

"I'll be checking in, but your mom's going to be fine."

"How do you know?"

"Because I'm *her* mom." She smiles. "You're not seeing eye-to-eye with each other right now, but give it time." She pauses. "You know, you can't change someone else. No matter how you try or what means you use. They have to want it for themselves. That's when it'll happen."

Somehow I think she's talking about more than just Mom. "So, basically, I should just let everything go? Worry about myself and that's it? Nothing matters because everything's just a drop of water?"

"Oh, no, no, no. You've got it all wrong. You *can* care." She slaps her leg. "Look at it like this: you can keep standing up for Sam—it's who you are—but don't use your fists. Even if you never get Bobby to change his mind, you're doing the right thing. Just a drop of water doesn't mean something insignificant."

"But you always say it when something's not a big deal."

She laughs. "Quite the opposite. It's from a song called 'Dust in the Wind.' Ever heard it?"

I shake my head.

"Well, you are missing out. Sit tight for a minute."

Grandma comes back from the other room with a CD in her hand. I put it in my CD player and we sit back on the bed.

She says, "It's one of the best songs of all time. I wish

your grandpa could have heard it, but it came out a few years after he passed."

"What's it about?"

"Listen. I mean, really listen." The song hums through the room and she closes her eyes and sways.

I get why she likes it. It's mellow and totally sucks me in. I hear the words *just a drop of water*, but I still don't get it because I'm pretty sure the song means the drop is one small drop in a giant ocean, which makes it not a big deal.

She opens her eyes when it's over. "So, what do you think?"

"I like it."

"That's it?"

I sink back into my pillows. "I don't know. I like it, but I don't get why you say 'just a drop of water.'"

She laughs. "It's all about interpretation. I think you're viewing that song the same way ninety-nine percent of people do. We're just one small thing in a great big universe. But I don't see it that way." Her eyes are almost glowing. "We are one small thing in a great big universe, but even one small drop of water can make a ripple in a giant ocean. A drop of water can help carve a canyon. One idea can chip away at another person's soul until they might just start believing that idea themselves. Everything in life is a big deal, sometimes just in the smallest of ways."

I like her interpretation of the song more than my own, so I'll hang on to that.

"Keep doing the right things and maybe you'll help carve a canyon for someone one day. Maybe you'll help change someone's mind, but if not, you're still part of this great big world. And that's a wonderful thing. Now, give me a kiss goodbye," she says as she stands.

She pulls me to my feet and kisses the top of my head. "I'll check in with you tomorrow. Love you."

I throw my arms around her. "I love you, too." I hug her extra tight because, to me, it's better than any verbal apology I could give her.

....

I think about what Grandma said for a long time. It's stupid to hang on to some fantasy about what I thought Grandpa was. So he didn't fight in a war. Big deal. He was in charge of keeping peace, of stopping wars before they started. If I'm being honest, it's actually pretty cool. I can see him dressed in a suit going to top-secret meetings with foreign leaders. He must've been really important. Then my mind flips to a picture of him being held in some prison. He's tied up, getting beaten, and then they pull out a gun.

I can't breathe. I've seen that stuff in movies, but

the pain was fake. For my grandpa, it was real. All of it hits me so quickly. Then I remember: the medal. I need his medal. I prop myself against the closet door and sit there for a long time. My eyes burn. I shut them to keep the tears from coming but when I do, I picture Mom crying. And then I see a thirteen-year-old version of her, along with Grandma, crying next to a grave. A funeral. Grandpa's funeral. Mr. Steiner's funeral. A flag. Grandpa's flag. I don't have the medal and my sudden need for his flag won't go away.

Mom's in the shower and Dad's in the kitchen. I head to the living room, snatch the flag out of the box on the mantel, and sneak back to my room. I tuck it under my pillow and wait for everyone to go to sleep so I can wrap myself in Grandpa's greatness. And maybe, just maybe, I'll feel okay again.

But I won't close my eyes tonight. I don't want to see those pictures in my head again.

CHAPTER 20
SEPTEMBER 26, 2001
WEDNESDAY

....

I listened to "Dust in the Wind" over and over until my alarm went off at six a.m. Maybe I'll never get Bobby to change, but it killed me not to put him in his place when he pulled out that pig and Muslim picture the other day. It's not like me to sit back and do nothing, but Grandma's right. I can't keep getting into trouble. I don't know how Grandpa kept peace—though I wish I did.

I made some other decisions last night, too. The FBI is full of smart people, but even smart people aren't perfect. They definitely got things wrong with Mr. Madina—immigration papers or not. I've known this all along, but maybe I just needed time for my head to agree with my gut. I'm going to talk to Uncle Hugh today, no matter what Mom says.

Even though I have no idea what's going to happen with Sam and me—I don't know how to forget everything that's happened between us—I don't want Aamber to think I meant those things I said. I definitely need to fix things with her.

....

I have to get to the store and back to our neighborhood in time to catch Aamber on her way to school, so I shower and dress as quick as I can, grab thirty bucks from the stash in my old pencil box, leave a note on my bed, and head outside.

The grocery store's pretty empty. I know I can get cherry Pop-Tarts, but I'm not sure they'll have any silly string. In the aisle with birthday cards and some toys, I find a box with four cans of assorted colors. Perfect. I grab all of them and stop by the Pop-Tart aisle on my way to the check-out.

Back home, both Mom and Dad are having breakfast. Mom's dressed for work, the first time in days. Maybe she *is* going to be okay, but that also means I'll have to call Uncle Hugh now before she gets there and answers the phone. I shove bacon in my mouth and grab the cordless phone as I head to the bathroom to brush my teeth. Uncle Hugh doesn't answer so I leave a message, on his voice mail, that I need to speak with him but not to call me back. I'll try again later. I hope he doesn't ask Mom about it.

....

I wait around the corner from the Madinas', in case Sam decides to make an appearance at school today. I have nothing to say to him right now. Finally, Aamber comes out alone. She looks a bit messy, like my mom's looked the last two weeks. Maybe I should leave. She probably won't talk to me anyway. I step into some tall bushes and wait for her to pass, but she sees me as she walks by.

"Jake?" She steps closer. "What are you doing?"

I didn't plan what to say. Instinctively, I bend and my hands fumble through the bag. I pull out a can of silly string and hand it to her.

She stares at it, and I can tell she's thinking hard. Only she doesn't say anything before turning and walking away.

I should have figured that would happen. I was a total jerk and made things worse when she's already got enough going on. I pick up my backpack and step from the bushes to brush the leaves off my clothes, but when I do, Aamber attacks me with the silly string and laughs her head off. As much as I hate that sticky, gooey feeling, I stand there and take it until the can is empty. Eventually, she loops her arm in mine and we walk to school together without saying much, but it feels good, silly string and all.

....

Thankfully there's no journal question this morning. Aamber fills me in that the class started working on the peace rally yesterday.

Mrs. Cruz announces, "Get into your groups, everyone. Bobby and Jake, you guys were out yesterday so pick a group and they'll fill you in. Those groups that haven't contributed an idea yet, keep brainstorming. We need something in the next few minutes."

Puzzled, I look at Aamber.

"Bobby had internal suspension yesterday for the pig thing," she tells me.

I can't help but smile.

"You can be in our group," she adds.

I'm glad he got in trouble and even more happy I had nothing to do with it. He's sitting with Rigo now, and they're basically their own group.

After ten minutes, Mrs. Cruz writes IDEAS on the board and underlines it. "Who wants to share one of their suggestions?"

No one raises a hand so she calls on Matt. "I dunno," he says. "Maybe a basketball game. Sports are competitive, but we could do it for fun. Not keep score or anything."

She writes BASKETBALL. "Fantastic. Sports can be a great way to show peace."

Katie raises her hand. "Jake said his grandpa got a paper crane from a kid overseas once and they're supposed to represent peace. We could have a station set up to make Origami cranes."

Why'd she have to mention my name with that?

Bobby busts out laughing. "That is the—"

"Do *not* say a single word unless it's an idea for our list," Mrs. Cruz says through clenched teeth. Bobby leans back in his seat and shuts his mouth.

Mrs. Cruz writes ORIGAMI CRANE on the board. "The paper crane is known as a symbol of peace all over the world. There's a legend that says if you fold a thousand of them, your heart's desire will come true."

She looks at me and it's like she wants to me say something. When I don't, she finally says, "I'm going to put you in charge of getting the paper for the cranes. Check with the art department to see if they have any to spare."

I know I'll have to do what she says, but I don't see how paper cranes will bring about peace in any way.

Especially with Bobby. Then again, it was enough for Grandpa to carry his around every day. Maybe it was the thing that kept him going, even if he had days when he wanted to give up. Maybe that crane was to Grandpa what Grandpa's medal is to me.

....

By the end of class, Matt had found a group on the Internet called Peace Players International. Their website gave some information on how to plan a basketball game as an "integrated event that would maximize the lesson of tolerance." Let's hope so, because Bobby signed up to play.

....

At lunch, Aamber, Katie, and Ian grab our usual table near the window in the cafeteria.

I've never seen Kirk in our lunch, so when I pass him on the way to my seat, I invite him to come sit with us. Then I say, "If you don't feel like being around anyone, we could go sit in the courtyard alone."

"We can sit with them," he says. "I'm tired of thinking too much."

I know exactly what he means.

As we start eating, Aamber turns to me and says, "I've been meaning to ask you, did you ever find that medal?"

I shake my head and tell them the whole story about Mr. Wilkey and the lost medal. Then I add, "What a whacko. I mean, really. The guy's a total nut, coming after me like that in the middle of the night."

Ian asks, "What were you doing out in the middle of the night?"

I lie. "I couldn't sleep and I wanted to be ready for the Palmetto meet so I figured I'd run." They all give me funny looks. "Anyway, now he's leaving me notes, newspapers, and Gatorade."

"You don't drink them, do you?" Katie asks.

I ignore her and turn to Aamber. "How does he even know I only like the green ones?"

Kirk looks annoyed. "So, go see him. That's what he wants. Why are you so afraid of him, anyway?"

Kirk's comment makes me feel dumb. "I'm not afraid of him. He's just so creepy and knows way too much about me."

Kirk mocks. "Do you hear yourself? *That's* messed up."

"Here, I'll help." Katie takes out a notebook and her hand flies across the page as she scribbles, *Mr. Wilkey,*

Sorry I can't meet you, but please leave the medal on your doorstep and I'll come get it tomorrow, Thursday, at 6 p.m. Thank you for keeping it safe. Jake

I grab the note and toss it back at her. "Duh, if I can come get the medal, then I can definitely see him."

She scribbles, *P.S. I can't stay, I have to be somewhere at 6:05.*

The bell rings and I haven't even touched my food. We get up, but before I leave, I turn around and grab the note. Just in case.

....

I run to find Aamber before she leaves school.

"Hey, can you do me a favor?" I pull out a note.

"For Sam?"

I fold the paper one more time. "For Mr. Wilkey, but I have practice, so can you leave it on his top step for me?"

"You want me to *go* there?"

"You're right. It's pretty risky."

She sighs and grabs the note from my hand. "Fine, I can do it."

I feel bad. I don't want anything to happen to her.

She tucks it in her backpack. "Is it Katie's note?"

"No, I wrote my own."

"You're not going to meet him, are you?"

I tug on my backpack strap. "I don't know yet. I'll see how he replies."

....

For the first time in weeks, I can't wait to get out and run. Running makes things feel like normal, almost, except that Sam's not here. And even though I don't want it to, it bothers me. Today's an easy day, the day before a race, so I run along the road in front of the school and down the street toward the mosque. Sam's out front with some other kids.

I jog over to them. "Hi."

Sam turns around. "What are you doing here?"

"Cross country practice. Look, we have a meet tomorrow. We need you."

"I can't. We're getting ready for an open house on Saturday."

"You're selling your house?" I'm in complete shock.

A man behind Sam laughs quietly as my mouth hangs open.

"No, an open house here at the mosque. We're inviting people to come and learn what true Islam is about."

My ears perk up. "Can I come?"

Sam looks away.

The man behind Sam steps forward. "Of course. We'd be delighted to have you." He looks at Sam. "I'm sure Sameed will give you the details."

Sam nods but doesn't look happy about it.

The man sticks out his hand. "*Salaam*. I'm Sheikh Muhammad Ibrahim."

I shake it. "I'm Jake."

Sam stares blankly at the ground.

The open house gives me an idea. "Maybe there's something else Sam can do, too, for the mosque . . . well, for your religion, I mean."

"Islam," the man says.

"Yeah, Islam."

Sam folds his arms over his chest.

I duck my head and try to catch his eye. "Our class is planning a Night of Peace at school. It's Friday night. We're trying to get people from different backgrounds to come and talk. Maybe you can talk about Islam."

Sam doesn't answer so Sheikh Muhammad does. "That's a wonderful idea. It will truly help deter the idea that Muslims are extremists." He looks at Sam. "The adults are hardest to convince, but you'll have a great audience to talk to, Sameed. You should help your friend."

Sam shakes his head. "That means I'd have to go to school on Friday. You should find someone else."

Sheikh Muhammad says, "You need to go to school. Your education is important."

Sam protests. "But we're getting ready for the open house!"

"You can help after school on Thursday and again on Saturday morning. It's time for you get back to your routine. We'll still be here."

"But . . . what about prayers?"

"You can do your noon prayers at school."

Sam hangs his head. "I still need to take care of my mom, but I'll think about it."

Sheikh Muhammad swings around to face me. "It was wonderful to meet you, Jake. I look forward to seeing you on Friday, if you don't mind my attendance at your rally."

"No, that'd be great. You can probably talk, too." I smile back.

He touches my shoulder gently, then walks away.

I grab my foot behind my back and stretch my leg. "Since you're thinking about the rally, maybe you could think about coming back to school tomorrow, too, so you can race."

Silence.

"Sam, you're gonna get in trouble for cutting classes."

"My mom excused the absences this morning."

"Well, the team needs you. You shouldn't let them down."

He looks away.

"Fine." I turn to leave, but anger burns my chest. "I'm sick of being ignored by you, you know. I stood up to Bobby for you. But you won't even stick up for yourself. Go ahead and hide from us all, Sam. I'm over it."

I take off in a sprint toward school. The air is hot in my lungs, but the pavement is smooth. There are no tree branches to swat away. No holes to look out for. Just open sidewalk. And even though I should feel free, it's more like I want to throw my hands up and surrender.

....

After practice, I push the locker room door open and head outside. I stop dead in my tracks when I see Mom waiting for me.

"Need a ride?" she asks.

"What are you doing here?"

We walk toward her car. "I had an appointment nearby and then went to the store. I figured I'd pick you up on my way home."

I climb into the car. She seems normal, like before-Sam-got-beat-up-normal and she asks, "How was school?"

"Good." I look out the window. Part of me thinks I should warn her now about the rally—she'll hear about it at some point anyway—but for the first time in a long time, she seems happy and I don't want to wreck that.

There's a note propped up on the Wilkeys' top step as we drive by.

"Mom, stop."

She slams the brakes. "What's wrong?"

"Sorry, it's just that I have to check in with the Wilkeys. I'll run home from here."

She gives me a funny look. "Okay, but come right home after."

I hop out of the car and she drives away.

My heart pumps fast.

Then I hear, "Jake."

I look around. Aamber's standing near her fence. I grab the letter from the step and sprint toward her.

"What are you doing here? He didn't come out when you left my note, did he?"

"No, but I was just checking to see if he took it when I saw you drive by. What's it say?"

I tear the envelope open. *I'd love to discuss the newspaper article with you. I hope you read it. The medal, and I, will be waiting for you.*

This is seriously crazy. "I'm going to have to go in. There's no other way. I just have to figure out when."

I stick the note back in the envelope. "Any more news about your dad?"

She shakes her head. "It's been eight days. My dad's boss came to see us this afternoon. He brought some groceries and chlorine for the pool. He helped Sam clean it and then visited with my mom, but he couldn't get her to snap out of her daze either."

"Is there anything I can do? I mean, I called my uncle today but he didn't answer." Maybe I need to find an excuse to see him in person.

"I just want to know where he is and that he's okay. It'd be a lot easier. I know he'll be back—they have no reason to keep him—but I never thought it would take this long."

I nod. "I'll see what I can find out. I've got to run, though. Want to walk to school tomorrow?"

"I'm going back to the MMS announcements tomorrow morning, so I'll just see you in class."

I can't help but smile. Finally, something's going back to normal.

CHAPTER 21
SEPTEMBER 27, 2001
THURSDAY

....

Dad shakes me. "Jake, get up. You're going to be late."

I pull the covers tighter around my neck, but he yanks them off.

"Get up. I forgot to wake you."

I look at the clock. It's eight twenty-five. Last night, I looked up Uncle Hugh's cell number in Mom's phone and called him, but he didn't answer. I was hoping he'd call back before school today.

"Where's Mom?"

"She left for work already. You need to hurry."

I throw on my Mangrove jersey and my Eagles hat, skip breakfast, and wait for Dad in the car.

I scan the sidewalks along the way, hoping to spot Sam. We need him to race today, but I don't see him, and even in school he's a no show again. Some teammate.

....

We spend the first twenty minutes of social studies class making sure everyone's on track for the event tomorrow.

Katie says, "I had a great idea last night. We should make buttons."

Mrs. Cruz adds BUTTONS to her list. "What kind?"

"They'll be red, white, and blue and read, UNITED WE STAND!"

I think about me and Sam, about Bobby, about Mom's feelings toward the Madinas, about the attacks, and about Mr. Madina being hauled away. We're definitely not standing united. What a joke!

I must've scoffed out loud because Mrs. Cruz looks at me and asks, "Is there something wrong, Jake?"

I shake my head.

"You're allowed to say something if you disagree."

I look at Katie. "No offense, but that's a stupid saying. We're definitely *not* united."

Katie puts her hands on her hips. "What planet do you live on? Haven't you been outside? Just look around. There are flags being sold on every street corner and practically every car and house has one flying from it. There are patriotic banners everywhere. Everyone's so nice to each other. Everyone stops to talk to each other. It's never been like that before."

I shake my head again. "I don't agree."

Bobby speaks up. "What Katie means is that *Americans* are united. Not everyone who lives here is an American."

Rigo snorts.

My stomach lurches. I try to shut out his voice and sit on my hands.

Mrs. Cruz eyes Bobby then says, "Katie, I like the idea, but let's take it a bit further. Do you know what the full saying is? It's not just 'united we stand.'"

Katie shakes her head.

Mrs. Cruz sits on the edge of her desk. "It comes from an old Revolutionary War song. I think the words went something like *hold hands brave Americans all, by uniting we stand, by dividing we fall*. The phrase is more like advice rather than a simple statement."

Katie nods. "Well, we can put the whole slogan on the button, then. It will tell people that we're asking them to stick together."

"Great!" Mrs. Cruz points to the board. "Now, let's draw names for our peace basketball teams. I've limited it to eighth graders only. The rest of the school can watch. If you signed up, your name's in the hat." She writes PEACE PLAYERS on one side of the board and FREEDOM FIGHTERS on the other.

I snicker quietly. Freedom Fighters for a peace rally? That's a good one.

When she's done, there are twelve kids in the first column. Matt and Rigo are both on the Peace Players team. The second column has eleven names. One is Bobby's.

Bobby stands and motions to the board. "Go ahead and put a star next to my name. I'll be the team captain."

I let out a *pfft* and Bobby's in my face instantly. He spits his words. "You think that's funny?"

For the fourth time, Mrs. Cruz steps between us. "That's enough."

He backs away. "I don't see your name up there, Jake. Too scared to play against me?"

Unlike all the past times, I feel nothing when he says this to me. He's not my enemy anymore. There is no war between us. I'm surrendering. "No, I'm not scared. I just don't care." I turn to Mrs. Cruz. "And, I'm staying with my grandma this weekend so I actually can't come to the rally."

Bobby doubles over with maniacal laughter. "So, you're gonna run and hide? I wonder if you'll sprint faster than Sam did when he left the park that morning."

Aamber and I both jump out of our seats, but it's

Aamber who yells at him, "Don't ever go near or talk about my brother again!"

"Out!" Mrs. Cruz grabs Bobby by the arm. "Now!"

The hair on my neck stands up. My heart is pulsing in my ears, in my throat, and in my wrists. I close my eyes, but all I see is Sam on the ground with blood oozing from his nose. I want to hit Bobby more than anything right now, but I think about Grandpa. This has to stop.

I rush to the board. "Fine, I'll play." I erase Rigo's name from the Peace Players and put him as a Freedom Fighter with Bobby. I add my name to the Peace Players team.

Bobby smirks. "So much for Grandma's."

Mrs. Cruz hands him a referral and sends him to the office.

The battle for peace is on. I'm pretty sure my literature teacher would call this an oxymoron.

....

In gym class, Coach Rehart unlocks the supply closet for me. "Get the bag of footballs and meet us at the field."

I grab the bag from the storage closet and am headed for the locker room bench when I hear Bobby's voice. "It'll be the perfect time. Everyone will be at the rally."

I thought he'd get in-school suspension when Mrs. Cruz kicked him out earlier, but I guess not. I hear a slap. A high-five? I slip back into the closet so he and whoever else is with him won't see me.

Rigo's voice bounces off the walls. "You don't think it's too close? There's gonna be cops all around the school."

Bobby says, "It's perfect that it's just down the street. We can show up here, slip out during the introduction, and be back before the game starts. No one will even know we're gone."

Rigo says, "What about the stuff?"

"We'll stash some of it in the bushes before the rally starts."

Rigo laughs. "We should get black ski masks, too."

I barely breathe. I'm afraid I might give myself away.

Bobby says, "That's cool. Much faster than face paint." There's silence for a second. "Do you have any masks?

Rigo says, "I can bring two."

"What about you?" Bobby asks.

No one answers. Who's he talking to?

I hear feet shuffling. "You in or what?" Bobby's voice booms.

"I don't know, man." *Matt?*

"Chickening out?"

"I never said I was in."

Shuffle, shuffle. A locker slams.

Bobby says, "You're such a loser. You better not say a word or I'll be at your house so fast."

I inch forward and steal a glance around a locker, hoping they don't plan to punch Matt because I'm not sure I'd be able to walk away.

Matt's backing away. "Look, I'm not gonna say anything. I just don't want to be part of it."

Bobby says, "Whatever. Let's get out of here before Coach comes looking for us."

I duck back into the supply closet. Bobby, Rigo, and Matt push through the metal door that leads to the track.

My pulse spazzes. *What are they up to?*

I shake my head. It doesn't matter. It's not my problem. I pace the closet floor. *Walk away. Let it go.*

I can't stay here at school. If I do, I'll get in trouble because all I want is to beat the lights out of Bobby till he tells me what he's planning. But I can't get involved. I have to get away. I escape out the back, over the school fence, and run through the park. I'm moving, but have no clue where to go. I remember Sam on the ground in this very spot and him walking away when Bobby hit him. I keep running, and unfortunately I keep thinking. The newspapers stated that the passengers on the

plane that crashed in Pennsylvania beat up the hijackers. They didn't just sit there; then again they were stuck
on the plane. Trapped. But what if they could have
walked away? Parachuted out and saved themselves?
I wonder if they would have, or if they'd still have fought
for what was right.

I run past the fire station. I jump over a bus stop bench
and dodge a crowd of people in front of the art museum.
Sweat pours down my face, but I don't stop until I'm in
front of City Hall, a solid four miles from school.

The Florida House of Representatives seal greets me
as I enter Uncle Hugh's office. Mom's chair is empty.
I hunch over and rest my hands on my knees as Uncle
Hugh comes out of his office.

"Jake?" He rushes at me. "What's the matter? Is
everything alright?"

I pant, "Yeah."

He leads me to a chair off to the side of the room
and brings me some water.

"I need you to help me with something. Please."

"Why aren't you in school?"

"You know my friend Sam? His dad was taken away
by the FBI. They're Muslim."

He exhales, long and slow. "I thought something
happened to you."

Once I can breathe normal again, I spill everything. "Look, my friend's dad needs help. He's been gone over a week and he didn't do anything wrong. I need to know if he's okay. And where he is. His family is so worried."

"I see. Is this why you called?" He sits in the chair next to me. "Why did they take him? If it's the FBI, I'm sure they had good reason."

"But that's it. They had no reason. Mr. Madina works at a bank. He was doing his job by helping Atta when he came into the bank for money. That's what he's supposed to do—help the customers. The FBI didn't arrest him for helping anyone else. They told his family it's because of his immigration papers, but I think that's just an excuse."

"It's probably more complicated than you think, Jake."

I throw my hands in the air. "Are you serious?"

"I didn't say I agree with it, only that it's probably complicated. We're in a different place now than we were three weeks ago. Everyone has a heightened sense of fear. Distrust. And it's hard to know who's been helping these terrorists along the way. It's the FBI's job to be thorough."

"But Mr. Madina didn't *do* anything wrong."

"Probably not. And they'll find that out."

I rest my head back on the wall and sigh. "When?"

He stands and heads toward his office. "Does your mother know you're asking me to help you with this?"

I look at the floor.

"Well, she's got enough on her plate right now." He shakes his finger at me. "I assume you're only asking me so that you can tell your friend's family that he's okay, right?"

I jump up. "I swear it!"

"Hang tight, then. Let me see what I can find." He closes his office door.

I want to stick my ear to the wall and listen, but he's the first person actually willing to help, so I go and sit quietly in Mom's chair and spin, counting the rotations. I used to be able to do seventeen. After only six spins, I grab her desk because the room is circling out of control. When my head clears, I happen to glance at her open calendar.

10:00 AM: Dr. Traynor.

I have no clue who that is. I flip back to the day before.

Wednesday 2:00 PM: Dr. Traynor

Tuesday 1:30 PM: Dr. Traynor

Monday 10:00 AM: Dr. Traynor corner of Sabal Palm and State Rd. 7 Suite 200

Is Mom sick? Dying? Is that why Dad took this week off and why Grandma stayed with us? Why didn't anyone tell me?

....

I need to get home. To find Mom. I jump from the seat.

Mom opens the front door to the office. "Jake! What—"

I run and throw my arms around her. "Mom, I'm sorry. I'm really sorry."

She pushes me back and inspects my face. "What's going on? Why aren't you in school?"

"Are you sick? Just tell me. I can handle it. I'll clean my room every day. And clean the house, too. You don't have to do anything. Just—"

She shakes me. "What are you talking about? I'm not sick."

"But your calendar says Dr. Traynor. And you went four times this week."

"Oh." She goes behind her desk and puts her purse away. "That. You shouldn't be reading my personal stuff. And why aren't you in school?"

"You can't ignore my question. Who's Dr. Traynor? Why did you go to the doctor's so many times?"

She smoothes her hair. "Because . . . because every-thing that's been going on lately is making me scared." She sighs. "More scared than usual." She taps the cal-endar. "Dr. Traynor is a therapist—a personal friend of Uncle Hugh's. He's trying to help me sort through things."

The tenseness in me fades. I hug her again, feeling a great sense of relief. When I let go, I look at her. "Is it working?"

She nods. "Well, it definitely feels good to talk about it. Maybe we should try that more at home, too."

"Does that mean we can talk about the Madinas again?"

Mom's lips pull into a thin line.

After a few minutes she says, "I know they're not bad people, but I still can't get involved. I just can't. You don't understand, but I need you to stop asking me to help them."

This is what Grandma meant. I can't make Mom be any different. "Alright, but how come you expect me to change? Sam's my best friend." *Or at least he was.*

"I don't. That wasn't fair of me." She sighs. "I'm not telling you to let this go anymore, and I will check in with Mrs. Madina soon, but I'm not getting involved with what's going on with Mr. Madina. It's the FBI's job, not mine. Deal?"

Shocked wouldn't even be close to describing what I feel. I make her shake on it before she changes her mind. "Deal."

She sighs. "I wish you could have met your grandpa."

I smile. "Yeah, me too."

Mom suddenly grabs my hand and says, "Some days I wish I'd never named you after him. It's so hard for me. I guess it wouldn't have mattered, though, because when I look in your face, I see him every single day. You're just as stubborn as I remember him being. But, mostly, you have his astute sense of right and wrong."

I'm almost speechless and let her words sink in, slowly. "I'm named after him? I thought his name was Richard."

"Richard Jake."

"Does it mean anything special?"

Mom looks right into my eyes. "Yeah, it means the greatest man who ever lived."

Forget supplanter. I'm named after the greatest man who ever lived. There's nothing better than that. And maybe I did replace someone after all.

"The difference, though, is your grandpa wouldn't be skipping school or getting in fights. You keep getting yourself into more and more trouble." She shakes her head.

"I know. I'm trying to fix that."

"We both have stuff to work on. It's going to take me a long time to get back to a good place. But I'm trying."

I hug her again. "Me too."

She squeezes me and then pulls back. "You can help me with one important thing tonight."

"Anything."

"What's the Madinas' favorite dessert? We've got some baking to do."

....

Uncle Hugh sticks his hands in his pockets as he comes out of his office. He looks at me and I think he's nervous about Mom being there.

She sorts the mail. "For goodness sake, Hugh. Tell the boy what he wants to know."

I brace myself. I always figured the FBI would realize Mr. Madina was innocent, but all of a sudden I feel sick. What if someone set him up and he looks too guilty for them to let him go?

Uncle Hugh says, "I don't know much right now. I put a call in to one of my colleagues, a senator in DC. Since this is a federal issue, she has more clout than I do. I explained the situation and she's going to check into it. I promise I'll let you know as soon as I hear anything." He comes over and gives me a hug. "You're a great friend. Sam's lucky to have you."

Yeah, well, Sam doesn't think so. I tell Uncle Hugh thanks as Mom grabs her keys. "Hugh, I'll be back in a few. I need to take Jake to school."

....

The lunch lady slops mashed up something on a bun and scoops pink carrots into the empty square on my paper tray. Disgusting. Sam would've had a funny comment about it endangering the human race or something. Man, I miss him. Matt is sitting by himself. I make eye contact and he nods at me. Bobby and Rigo are a few tables away, and I wonder if they ditched Matt because of what happened in the locker room.

I walk toward him. "Can I sit here?"

He stands. "Sure. I was just leaving. I . . . I have to meet Mrs. Cruz to help her with something for tomorrow night."

"Never mind, then." I turn around and head to my usual table.

....

Coach Rehart hands me an envelope when I get to the locker room after school. "Someone left this for you in the front office."

In the top corner is printed *Representative Hugh M. Baldwin*. I rush to my locker before I rip it open:

Jake,

There was a misunderstanding—something about his immigration papers—but everything's been cleared up. Mr. Madina should be home sometime this weekend. I promised I'd let you know as soon as I heard something.

Uncle Hugh

I shove my face inside my locker. My throat burns and my nose's clogged. I fumble around for a shirt. A towel. Anything. I cover my eyes and it takes everything in me not to sob out loud with relief.

He's coming home.

. . . .

"Coach," I crack his office door open. "I promise I'll be quick, but there's something I need to do."

He raises his eyebrows. "We have a meet today."

"It's for Sam."

Coach takes a deep breath and nods. "When you see him, tell him we want him back."

"I'll be fast. I promise."

. . . .

I approach the open doors of the mosque. I'm not sure

if I'm allowed in so I just stand there. Sam is walking barefoot with a rug rolled up under his arm. He comes toward me and grumbles, "What are you doing here?"

I grab the note from my shorts. A few days ago, I would have given anything to be there when Sam found out his dad is okay, but things have changed. I hand him the letter. "Please make sure you tell Aamber, too."

I start to leave, then turn around. "Oh, and Coach wants you to come back." I catch his eyes. "And so do I."

Then I take off as quickly as I came.

I get back as Coach is finishing his talk with the team. "You can win this. Stay focused." He looks at me. "Here." He hands me Sam's captain band.

"No, thanks, Coach. Sam will be back eventually. Kirk can lead alone today."

Kirk claps me on the back. "You're solid!"

We pile our hands in the middle of the huddle. "Mangrove on three. One, two, three—"

"Mangrove!"

Mom and Dad wave to me as they walk toward the small crowd of fans.

The runners from all three teams step up to the chalk and I'm feeling nervous as I toe the line. I feel *off*, but the gun doesn't wait for me to get a grip before it sounds and I'm pulled ahead by the crowd around me.

After the first few turns, I'm making okay time, but there are three guys ahead of me. I try not to focus on them. I need to clear my head or I'll mess up for sure. All I can think about, though, is Sam. I never thought we'd stop being friends.

I pass the first stat girl. She yells my time and it brings my head back into focus. I'm forty seconds over my usual mark. But why be normal now? Nothing's been normal for the last few weeks. My mind skips to the Night of Peace and the open house at the mosque. I doubt any of it will make a difference.

I feel a runner sneaking up on me and shake everything out of my head. *Focus!* I pass the second timer and I've gained fourteen seconds, but I'm still behind three of the Flamingo runners and one kid from Dolphin Bay who has somehow passed by without me even seeing him. Kirk's in the lead, thankfully.

My pace is steady. I can't keep guessing how Grandpa would handle the stuff with Bobby. It hurts my head. I now know another reason why I hate cross country, besides the holes and branches: there's too much time to think.

I pass the kid from Dolphin Bay who's holding his side as he slows to a jog. The finish line's up ahead. I can see it. Kirk's about to pass through it in first place. The three runners in front of me sprint to the yellow tape, but I have to do this for Sam. For Kirk and Grandpa and Coach and . . . for me. I want to do this for me. I push myself more than ever. I pump harder and stretch longer with each step and pass two runners. The funnel squeezes and I cross the finish line in third place.

Dad's clapping loudly. I think he even shouts, "Woo hoo!" Though I'm slightly embarrassed, I'm glad he's here to see me race for once.

I started out horrible but pulled through in the end. Maybe that's all that matters. I bend over, resting my hands on my knees, and pant while the last of the runners cross the finish line.

Coach comes over. "A great run, Jake, especially after your little sprint to see Sam earlier."

"Thanks." The mention of Sam spirals my thoughts again and I feel anger rising in my chest as I realize I kept expecting Sam to come through and show up on the course during the race.

As if he's reading my mind, Coach says, "I'm sure Sam will be back before our next meet."

But that's just dumb, because it's pretty clear to me that Sam's never coming back.

....

Mom sticks the apple pie we made into a box and I take

it over to the Madinas'. I don't ask her to come with me. I'm just glad she made it at all.

When I ring the bell, Aamber opens the door and throws her arms around me. "He's coming home. Thank you so much, Jake."

"I didn't do anything. You would have found out soon enough."

"Still, thanks for asking your uncle after all. And for going to tell Sam as soon as you found out. He called us right away but still hasn't come home. I don't know what's going on with him."

She takes the pie from me and grabs the newspaper from under my arm. "Is this what Mr. Wilkey wanted you to read?"

I nod. "Page ten. I don't get it though."

She scans the article. "Me either. You going over there now?"

"Yeah." I want to ask her for a paper bag in case I start hyperventilating because I'm pretty sure I'm about to. *Breathe. In. Out.* "I need to get it over with."

....

Aamber walks with me to the Wilkeys' yard. "Sure you don't want me to go in with you?"

I don't think I'll ever be able to pull another prank on her again. "No, but thanks."

My heartbeat vibrates though my bones as I edge closer to the porch. I'm not sure if it's fear or guilt that's making me so shaky. I make it to the top step and then turn around. Aamber gives me a thumbs up. I force a smile. Facing the door, I bring my hand up to knock, but, before I can, the door opens wide.

My gut lurches like an old cannon. I don't see anyone at first. Then a sheet-white hand appears from behind the door. It's holding Grandpa's medal. I could just snatch it and run. I mean, I read the article. I came over. I did what he asked. But nothing will change if I don't go inside. I take a breath and step through the doorway.

The lights are turned low. It takes a few seconds before I can see. Mr. Wilkey's face isn't as scary as I remember from that night in the rain. It's actually worse. His skin has moon-craters and is sunburned. His nose looks like it has a swollen brain stuck on the tip. I feel bad for him and try not to look him in the eyes when I take the medal from his hand.

"Glad you came, Jake," he rasps.

I shiver. My fingers are sweating so I stick them in my pockets, along with the medal, to wipe them without Mr. Wilkey noticing.

He points toward the living room. "Have a seat."

I inch my way in. There are family pictures all over the walls. Mr. Wilkey looks normal in most of them, though there are a few of him and Mrs. Wilkey with some kids in them who don't seem bothered by his face at all. I move farther into the room. Over the piano there's a wedding photo and I noticed that Mr. Wilkey's in uniform. A Navy uniform. I look from the picture to him. He catches me and I dart my eyes back to the wall.

"I'd like to say those were the good old days, but two weeks after our wedding, the Japanese hit us at Pearl Harbor." He sits in a tall, cushioned chair. "Didn't get to see my bride for quite some time after that."

I pull the medal out of my pocket and sit across from him in a matching chair. "Pearl Harbor?" I suddenly forget all about being scared. I've never heard a real war story or met a real soldier. "You were at Pearl Harbor when it was attacked?"

"I was making my way back from the infirmary." He points to his swollen face. "I've had this skin condition most of my life. It's called rosacea. It wasn't bad back then—just got a little wind-burned now and again. Even managed a landscaping business after I got out of the military, but eventually the sun became too much. Anyway, I had just picked up some cream when the first planes flew over. I was close enough to my sub that I was able to man the guns within minutes."

"Whoa, you were on a submarine?"

"Yes, sir, the *USS Dolphin*. We were moored port-side to pier four, but unfortunately were too far away for our small guns to really hit anything. We got lucky the Japanese didn't hit the sub port, though, or it might've changed the war completely. We were able to get back underwater the very next day. Our sub fleets did a lot of damage to the Japanese vessels over the course of the war, which helped cut off trade in and out of Japan."

My eyes are bugging out, I can feel them. I can't believe he fought in an actual war. "Did your submarine ever sink a ship?"

"You say that with such a spark in your eye. Did you read the newspaper article I gave you?"

"Yeah."

"And what did you think of it?"

I sink back into the chair and clench Grandpa's medal. "I don't know." And I really don't. The whole newspaper changed my world. It taught me something about Kirk's dad, Atta, Allah, the *Qur'an*. It made me doubt Sam's family. Only not really. I guess I did that myself.

He taps the column. "It says right here, it's ignorant to think you can judge a man's soul by looking at his face."

"Yeah, I read that. That's what my mom did to Sam's

family, actually. She judged them even though she knew them."

"Well, sometimes fear kicks in and we become irrational."

"Yes." I slap the arms of the chair. "She was irrational. That's the word I've been looking for."

He looks at me. "And you?"

I pull back. "Me? What about me? I'm not afraid. I stood up for Sam. If I were old enough to join the military, I'd sign up today. I'm definitely not afraid, and I'm definitely rational."

"You're afraid of me." He says it so plainly.

"Yeah. I mean no. But . . . well, my mom *knows* the Madinas. She wasn't rational at all."

I didn't know Mr. Wilkey. You know how people say their lives flash before their eyes right before they die? That's how I feel because clips of The Albatross flick in my head. Katie. Kirk's voice ringing in my ears asking me why I'm so afraid of the Wilkeys. I close my eyes to make it all slow down. And then it's clear. He's right. Sam was right, too, because I am just like Mom in a way.

My throat's so dry I can't talk. I cough and try to find words.

Mr. Wilkey goes to the kitchen and brings back a green Gatorade.

I gulp half of it in one shot.

He grabs the newspaper from the side table and hands it to me. "Read the last two paragraphs."

I read them before. It's like what the priest at church said—it's okay to be angry. But, when I read the lines this time, it seems a lot clearer: that anger can lead us to a place of hatred and intolerance. And, if we get to that point, then everything that really matters is already lost.

Mrs. Cruz sorta said the same thing about me hitting Bobby. And Coach Rehart, too. I look at Mr. Wilkey.

"Jake, I saw war. It's ugly. It's real. People die. I have friends who didn't make it back. Heck, I should be dead, too. War comes from hate and that starts inside us. That includes one punch here or there. It's all a type of war."

I leap from my seat. Grandpa's medal goes flying. "But someone has to pay! It's not fair for them to get away with it. Not Bobby. Not the hijackers. Do you think the Japanese should have gotten away with Pearl Harbor?"

"No, and they didn't. I'd go back and fight again if I had to—to defend our freedom. But sometimes fighting isn't the only answer. If you can find another way to solve a problem, do it. Trust me." He picks up the medal and hands it back to me. "I think your grandfather would agree."

How does he even know about Grandpa? Or that I hit Bobby? Or that I like green Gatorade? How does he know anything about me?

"My grandpa's dead so the whole peace thing didn't really work out for him," I yell as I run for the door without looking back. He doesn't try to stop me.

....

Aamber's in the same spot when I left her. "I've been freaking out. Are you okay?"

I storm by her. I'm sick of hearing the same thing over and over. Everyone says not to fight, but no one wants to tell me how to win this war with Bobby.

"Wait!" She grabs my arm. "Did you get the medal?"

I pull it from my pocket and walk right past her. All the way home.

....

I shove my homework in my backpack and pull out *The Art of Origami* that Mrs. Cruz lent me. The bright paper squares are stacked in a neat pile on my desk. I take one, but the directions and illustrations in the book are like a Martian language.

I give up and instead grab a pencil and scribble on a red paper square all the things Bobby and Rigo could be planning:

1. *Egg Sam's house*
2. *Egg my house*
3. *Beat Sam up*
4. *Something with the game*
5. *Rob a bank*
6. *Mr. Madina . . .*

My palms sweat. There's no way Bobby could know *that?* But maybe he has connections just like Uncle Hugh.

Oh, man! I really hope Mr. Madina *doesn't* come home tomorrow.

CHAPTER 22
SEPTEMBER 28, 2001
FRIDAY

....

Mom opens my blinds and says, "Good morning, honey."

I stretch.

"Hurry up so you have time to eat. I'm making French Toast."

It's like my old mom is back, but at the same time, I know we're both different somehow. It's not necessarily a bad thing, though.

I hop out of bed and dress quickly. Bobby and Rigo are up to something and I'm pretty sure it involves the Madinas—especially if Bobby found out Sam's dad is coming home. Their house isn't far from the school and Bobby did say something about payback. They're probably going to set something up at Sam's for when his dad returns. If Mom comes to the rally, it'll be hard for me to escape and follow them. I have to convince her to stay home.

"Mom, are you coming to the rally tonight?" I ask as I enter the kitchen.

"I wish I were as brave as you." She sighs. "And I wish I could be there for you. But I don't think I can. I'd be a mess. I'm just not ready."

"Think you'll ever be ready?"

"I hope so. But don't hold me to it, okay?"

I remember my and Sam's promise when we traded the G. I. Joe figures, that we'd be "friends till Martians invade the earth." Lately, promises seem like empty words. Kind of like saying sorry. I don't hold Sam to that promise anymore. And I won't hold Mom to hers either. But at least she's trying.

....

I begged Dad to take me to school early so I could find Aamber. Once I get there, I dart for the MMS TV room.

It's like she's still floating with the news of her dad and she gives me another big hug. It's nice. Really nice. But this is important so I push the feeling from my mind. "Who have you told about your dad?"

She tilts her head in confusion. "Just Katie and Ian."

"Listen to me. You can't tell anyone else. Not yet. Okay?"

"Why not? You're kinda freaking me out."

"Just trust me. I think Bobby's up to something and I need to find out what it is."

Her eyes grow big. "Are they going to hurt my dad?"

"No, I doubt it. But I don't want them to know he's coming home. Let me find out what they're planning first. It'll probably be something at the rally instead, but I just want to be sure."

"I trust you. You better let me know if you plan to get yourself in trouble again, though. Bobby's not worth it, remember?"

I can't promise that, so I don't. I fought Bobby before and it didn't change anything so maybe there *is* another way.

She folds her arms over her chest. "So, are you going to tell me what happened with Mr. Wilkey?"

"Sorry I took off. He just knows so much about me and I got creeped out." I fill her in quickly.

"Does he look as bad as everyone says?"

"Worse. I actually feel bad for him. He has some skin problem so he doesn't go out in the sun much or his face gets all swollen and itchy. But he's got family—even grandkids—and seems pretty normal."

She laughs. "I guess the legend of the vampire is officially over."

"Yeah, I guess so."

....

In social studies, everyone's working on their projects for the rally. I get stuck making paper cranes with Bobby because Mrs. Cruz wants us to call a truce.

He flops into the chair next to mine. As soon as she's gone, he says with a giant smirk on his face, "You ready for tonight?"

I look him dead in the eyes. "Yeah, I'm ready."

He laughs. "So you think." He grabs the book from my desk and picks up an orange square. He folds, tucks, creases.

I wish I could read his mind—to figure out what he plans to do at Sam's house.

He turns the book upside down, then sideways. Five minutes later, his bird looks like a fork. "This is stupid."

At least we agree on that.

"Rigo." Bobby motions him over.

Mrs. Cruz walks by. "Great, Rigo. You can help them. Have a seat."

Bobby laughs. "Yeah, good luck."

Rigo pulls a yellow square from the stack and starts folding without even looking at the book.

Bobby and I stare, mouths open.

Rigo shrugs. "What? My little sister likes to make 'em. I help her sometimes."

I try to fold the lines the same way he does, buying time and hoping they'll talk. Hoping they'll slip up and say something about tonight. But they don't.

I finally say, "Are you bringing your sister to the rally?"

Rigo shoots me a look like I'm the dumbest person in the world. He shifts in his seat and stares at the perfectly creased crane in his hand. "Of course not. It's the last place I want her to be." He cracks up and says, "Well, the second to last."

Bobby flicks him on the head.

He's gonna spill for sure. "Why?"

He leans back in his chair. "Because it's no place for her."

I point to his crane. "But it's a peace rally."

He rips the crane in half. "You're so stupid. No one's buying into this peace stuff."

Bobby stands. "Let's go back and work on our plays."

Rigo follows him.

It would've been too easy to find out like that. I need to step it up.

···········

When the lunch bell rings after fourth hour, I can't get to the cafeteria fast enough. I scan the room for Matt. It's risky, but I only have a few hours to figure out what Bobby's up to and Matt could be my only chance. I spot him coming out the lunch line door.

I walk fast to catch up without making it obvious. "Hey."

He looks at me. "Hi."

I shouldn't ask. He'll tell Bobby that I know something's up. "There's a table over there. Want to sit?"

He stops walking. "Listen, I—"

I face him. "I get it. Okay? We're not friends anymore. Fine. But I need to ask you something." Sweat drips down my forehead. He's gonna bust me for sure.

"What?"

I look around. Bobby and Rigo are still in line. "I know Bobby's planning something tonight."

He inspects his food tray. "I don't know what you're talking about."

"Yes, you do. I heard you guys in the locker room yesterday."

His face turns red as he scans the room. He walks toward the doors that lead to the courtyard. I keep up with him.

He pushes the door handle and we're outside.

"Stop following me."

I get in front of him. "I know Bobby threatened you so you wouldn't tell anyone. I heard it all. I won't even say you told me. I'll just show up. But, you have to tell me."

He looks at me. "I don't know anything. Now leave me alone." He steps around me and slips into the crowd.

I'm betting he gives Bobby a heads up that I know, but if Bobby comes after me, I'll be ready.

For the rest of the day, I brace myself every time I turn a corner, waiting for Bobby to pounce on me, but I make it to my next class. And the one after.

. . . .

I've got to follow Bobby after school. It could be my only chance, so I make my trip to see Mrs. Cruz quick. Time's running out. She hands me a paper. "This is our agenda. You'll do the welcome and then introduce Sheikh Muhammad."

"Okay." I show her my introduction and she nods. "I'll see you there." I rush for the door.

"Hold on. Gina's got some of the NJHS kids to run the origami table so you can stay up at the podium with me."

No! I can't go AWOL if I'm at the podium.

Someone will notice. "But, I practiced all day in my classes and I can finally fold them now. I need to teach people how—"

"Gina's got it covered. I need to you introduce Representative Baldwin after the Sheikh."

I've got to find a way out of podium duty. And I need to get out of here now before Bobby takes off.

Mrs. Cruz grabs her bag and walks into the hallway with me. "Can you be there at six?"

"Sure." This bites. I can still ditch the rally and just hide out in front of the school till Bobby tries to escape. Someone else can do the talking. But Matt will notice. If he hasn't said anything to Bobby yet, he still might. There has to be another way. Bobby's bike's already gone once I get outside. I need to warn Sam.

....

I hear Sam in his backyard and let myself in the gate while he tests the chlorine levels in the pool.

He looks up. "Hey."

"Hi."

"I'm getting ready to leave in a second, but thanks, you know, for the info about my dad."

"No problem. Look, you may not want to be friends

anymore, but I'm only here because something's going down tonight. Bobby and Rigo are up to something. I can't figure out what, but I'm pretty sure it involves you. Or at least your family."

The door to the Wilkeys' shed creaks on the other side of the fence. It's still daytime, so I assume Mrs. Wilkey must be feeling better.

Sam stands. "How do you know?"

I want to yell, *Because while you've been all mad and blowing me off, I've been battling with Bobby.* Instead I say, "I heard them in the locker room."

"What did they say?"

"Something about payback, and you, and ski masks. Whatever it is, it's happening tonight. I think they're gonna do something to your house."

He sets the chlorine tester on the patio table. "I won't let them." The look in his eyes tells me everything. Sam's back. I smile, as wide as that momma gator.

He adds, "But we can't fight them. Or, at least I won't. Not physically."

I reach in my pocket and touch Grandpa's medal. "I know. I have an idea. But it'll take two of us to pull off."

....

There are only five minutes till the rally starts when Mrs. Cruz leads me to the stage. "Jake—"

"Wait." I stop and look around. Bobby and Rigo are camouflaged by the crowd. I stand on my tiptoes, trying to get their position.

"Come on," she pulls me forward. "It's almost time to start."

My stomach churns as she leads me toward the podium. I bolt onto the stage and scan the crowd. Then I spot them. They're making their way toward the doors, then stop and stand against the back wall. Sam's beside Sheikh Muhammad on the gym floor below me. I grab his arm and he hops on the stage with me.

We don't take our eyes off Bobby and Rigo.

Mrs. Cruz reaches up and taps me. "Go ahead and start."

The microphone squeaks when I turn it on and people cover their ears.

"Sorry." I grab for my speech, but it's not in my pocket. My hands dig into the other pocket. Gone. I start to sweat. My mouth's dry. I can't look down in case I miss Bobby and Rigo's escape. My hand brushes over Grandpa's medal and I catch my breath. I can do this. Sam and I can do this.

I decide to wing the speech. "Uh, thanks for coming. We're in Mrs. Cruz's first period class. We wanted to have a peace rally . . ."

Bobby's saying something in Rigo's ear.

The gym lights are bright. I can't see clearly. I squint and focus on the back of the room. "We wanted the peace rally to show how . . ."

Rigo nods. They start moving. Sam pokes me in the side.

I wipe the sweat from my face. "Yeah, so we're doing a peace rally to promote peace." I shield the lights with my hand. The two of them are closer to the door now. "Uh, so I want to . . ." We need to go. Now. I look behind me. "I want to introduce Sheikh Muhammad. From the mosque down the street."

The crowd claps.

Then it hits me and I'm screaming in my head. Bobby and Rigo aren't going to Sam's and they aren't going to do anything to Mr. Madina either.

The Sheikh's on stage with Sam and me. He shakes my hand, then Sam's. A reporter snaps our picture. My heart is pounding out of my chest.

I pull Sam aside. "Change of plans. I know where they're going."

We jump off the stage. Once we're down, we scramble through the thick crowd and are outside in seconds. I don't see Bobby. Or Rigo. But if I'm right, they're headed to the mosque.

....

We run—faster than I've ever run in my life. We don't talk; there's no time, but we both know. Bobby. Rigo. Mosque.

We take the back way, hoping to get there before Bobby and Rigo do so we can cut them off. What are they gonna do? What are *we* gonna do? Sweat pours off me and my shirt's soaked. When we get to the mosque, there's no one outside. We either beat them here, or maybe I was wrong. Maybe they went to Sam's house after all. I put my hands on my head and take a deep breath. Then, two black shadows zip down the street. My heart squeezes. *Is this what it feels like going into battle?* We're not armed and I'm still not sure how to win without weapons. *Breathe.*

One street light shines overhead, but it's not bright enough for us to see what they're up to.

I hear, "Shhh." And maybe laughter?

They're getting closer. *Clank, clank, clank.*

Part of me thinks we should hide till we figure out what they're doing and yet, instinctively, I step into the glow of the street lamp at the same time Sam does. Our backs are to the mosque.

Clank. Clank. Then the noise stops and the two figures freeze.

My fist tightens around the medal in my pocket. "We know it's you. Bobby. Rigo. You can take off your stupid masks."

Bobby peels his off. Rigo doesn't.

Bobby takes a step toward us. "Here comes Jake again, defending the camel jockeys." He slaps Rigo in the gut.

Rigo doesn't laugh. Bobby grabs a black garbage bag from Rigo's hands. *Clank.*

"Go back to the rally. Whatever you're planning to do here is only gonna get you in serious trouble." I eye the bag.

Bobby reaches in it, pulls out a can of spray paint, and hands it to Rigo. "Us, get in trouble?"

Bobby walks toward the bushes near the sidewalk and slides a cardboard box out from under it and into the glow cast by the street light. He lifts one of several glass soda bottles and flicks a white paper towel sticking out of the top. "My dad wouldn't call this trouble. He'd be proud of me."

Sam whispers under his breath. "Oh, man. This is bad."

Rigo cocks his head and leans in, examining the bottle Bobby's holding. He reaches out to touch it, but Bobby pulls it away.

Sam steps closer to them. "What are you gonna do with those?"

Bobby smiles in the darkness. "Thought we'd have a little bonfire while we contribute some art work to this dump. I hear they're having people over tomorrow."

Sam and I inch over so we're between them and the mosque. I straighten. "You're gonna have to get around us first."

"Ha!" Bobby turns to Rigo. "Hear that, Rig? They think they can stop us."

Rigo eyes the bottle in Bobby's hands and takes a step back.

I glare at Rigo. "Is this why you didn't want your sister to come tonight? You didn't want her to see what you're really up to?"

He still has his ski mask on so I can't read his face, but his chest is moving up and down fast. Then faster.

Bobby says, "Don't listen to him, Rigo. We need to show these towel-heads that we don't want them in our city. Or in our country." He looks over my shoulder.

There's a shadow up ahead at the next street light. Then it's gone. Did Matt decide to help them?

Bobby yells at Rigo. "Come on! We need to show them they're not welcome here."

Rigo shakes his head.

Bobby reaches back and yanks him forward. "You're not chickening out, are you? You want them living near us?"

Rigo doesn't move or say anything.

Bobby gets in his face. "You like that your sister lived in the same building as Atta?"

Rigo tugs and stretches the collar of his shirt.

"Huh?" Bobby eggs him on. "You like that she knocked on his door to sell him a magazine for school?"

Rigo rips his mask off and shakes his head furiously. There's nothing but hate in his eyes as he steps forward and gets in Sam's face. "You're all terrorists!"

His words hover, thick like the air. My friend Rigo is gone. For good.

Sam doesn't flinch, though. He's calm as he points to the bag. "No, that would be you."

"They," I say, pointing to the mosque, "didn't kill anyone."

"They," says Bobby as he inches forward, "will pay."

He raises the bottle.

Everything moves in slow motion.

Bobby pulls a lighter from his pocket, lifts it to the

paper towel, and ignites it. He chucks the bottle at the wall of the mosque.

Sam sprints toward the building. Even if he catches it, it'll blow up in his hand. The bottle's airborne and it's faster than he is. *Crash.* Glass shatters just under the window and I shield myself from it and the fire.

I open my eyes, but don't see Sam. I scream and run toward the flaming bushes. Someone grabs my arms from behind. I struggle to break loose and charge forward again. I have to help Sam.

"Jake!" Someone clamps around my chest. "It's me. I'm right here." Sam shakes me.

I turn my head to look at him. Then at the fire. Then back at him.

He releases me from his grip.

We spin around. Rigo's eyes are filled with . . . fear? The can of spray paint is at his feet.

Bobby looks like he's in a trance, watching the fire torch the bush.

Sam steps toward Bobby. "Feel better now?"

Bobby snaps out of it, looks at Rigo, and slaps him on the back. "Ha. Not yet." He reaches into the box again.

The box. I lunge forward and scoop it up, but not before Bobby grabs another bottle.

He lights the paper towel, then hurls the bottle. Glass

shatters. More popping. I turn around. Flames creep up the outside wall of the mosque.

I smash the bottles on the sidewalk before they can be lit just as Sam pins Bobby to the ground.

We watch the flames reach a window. Bright orange. Angry.

Towers.

Fire.

Planes.

Fire.

Pentagon.

Fire.

Mosque.

Fire.

Feet running. People yelling. Flashlights flicker. Cops.

Someone's arms clench me and pull me from my daze. It's Mr. Wilkey and I feel an immediate sense of relief. Finally.

....

The firemen reel their hoses back onto the truck.

When the police finish asking me questions, I sit on the bench outside the mosque.

Dad hugs me for the tenth time. "I'm so glad Mr. Wilkey called me."

How did Mr. Wilkey know? I look for him in the crowd, but he's still being questioned. He risked showing his face to help me—to help us.

Dad and I walk to him. I smile and say, "Thanks," extending my hand to him.

Mr. Wilkey shakes it. "You know, despite the heat pricking my face, I've enjoyed watching and listening to you and Sam play soldiers over the years, especially when you planned attacks on Old Vampire Wilkey."

My eyes bug out and my voice disappears when I try to speak. I'm sure my cheeks are red.

He laughs and his swollen nose jiggles. "Never mind that. I knew you'd figure out what Bobby was up to. But, I had to follow you, just in case it got out of control."

Having fought in a war, it doesn't surprise me that Mr. Wilkey had a plan. I guess he's not so creepy after all.

The three of us watch as two cop cars pull away— one with Bobby in it; the other with Rigo.

Even after I told the cops what I could, none of this seems real.

Sam approaches me.

Dad shakes his hand and says, "We'll leave you two to talk."

Sam rocks back and forth. "I know you probably

don't want to be friends anymore, but I still have to say thanks again."

I *do* want to be friends, but I'm not sure it'll ever be the way it once was. There's still one thing I can't make sense of and maybe I never will, but I have to ask. "I do want to be friends, but I can't figure out why you never told me about your dad."

Sam looks at the street light and blinks quickly for a few seconds. He sighs and says, "Honestly, it's because I was embarrassed by him. Or it. I mean, you and I always talked about being soldiers and fighting for our country, but my dad wasn't even a US citizen. I wanted him to be and he always promised he would, but things got in the way, like him going back to school, working at the bank, and stuff like that. I didn't want you to see me any different because of it, so I decided not to tell you."

Never in a million years would I have guessed that Sam was embarrassed of his dad. But I get it, and I feel bad for him wanting to hide something like that from me—from everyone.

Sam looks me right in the eye when he says, "I really am sorry." And I know he means it.

I stare at his face. It's different—at least to me. For the first time I see Sam, a Muslim. An American Muslim. But he's still just Sam, no matter what.

I nod. "Me too."

He smiles. "You mean you still want to be friends?"

I smile back. "Yeah, but only till Martians invade the earth."

....

Dad's waiting for me at the curb. He puts his arm around me. "I owe you an apology."

"What for?"

We head back to the school to get his car.

"For not standing up to Bobby's dad a few weeks ago. I should have." He runs his hand though his hair. "I figured I couldn't change a man like that anyway, so why bother. I thought it was best to be polite and not make waves." Then he laughs.

I look at him. "What's so funny?"

He puts his arm around me. "Think about it. People like Dale Brinkmann do stupid stuff like this because they're afraid. And we let them get away with it because we're afraid, too. Ironic, right?"

"Yeah."

"But not you. You're brave. You and Sam both."

We were pretty brave, though I was scared, too. I never realized you could be both at the same time. I bet that's how Grandpa felt.

The trees form a canopy over the sidewalk. The sky's

filled with stars and the moon is almost full. The light stretching behind all the leaves above casts a whole lot of shadows, but they don't scare me at all.

....

We tell Mom about the mosque. Dad and I agree she doesn't need to know that I was there, though, at least not yet. I should be happy that he and I share this secret. It must mean he doesn't see me as a little kid anymore. But for some reason, part of me wishes that the biggest problem in my life was still the potholes and tree branches on the cross country course. Or not getting named team captain.

CHAPTER 23
SEPTEMBER 29, 2001
SATURDAY

....

Word spreads fast. The front lawn of the mosque is scattered with posters. Some have peace signs. Others read TEACH TOLERANCE. And there are flowers strewn everywhere, like people picked them right from their gardens and laid them on the lawn. A board covers the window that the fire shattered, and on the sidewalk there are people with other posters on sticks that read phrases like STOP ISLAMIC COLONIZATION: GET RID OF MOSQUES IN AMERICA and END THE WAR ON TERROR BY GETTING RID OF MUSLIMS. The battle will probably go on forever, but Sam and I will keep fighting, peacefully.

Just a drop of water.

Dad and I go around to the back of the mosque.

There are a few tents with food set up in the parking lot. Sheikh Muhammad comes over and shakes our hands.

"Jake," he says, "We're very grateful to you and Sam." He looks at me square in the eyes. "It takes a lifetime of courage to do what you two did." He turns to Dad and says, "You should be very proud."

Dad messes my hair. "Oh, I am!"

Sheikh Muhammad points to some chairs set up outside the entrance to the mosque. "Have a seat. We're just about to start."

There are at least a hundred people gathered. Aamber stands and waves us over to her and Mrs. Madina. They both hug us as we take our seats. I look and see Sam sitting up front. He waves, and I smile back.

I whisper to Aamber, "Is your dad back yet?"

"No, but I think it'll be today. I can feel it." She squeezes my arm. She's been the strongest one through all of this—even stronger than Sam or me and we've always called ourselves soldiers. I'm glad she and I are friends now, but I wish it hadn't taken all this for me to realize she's pretty cool.

Sheikh Muhammad steps up to the podium. "Welcome, friends. We deeply appreciate that you've come to our open house today. Our country experienced a great tragedy on September 11 at the hands of radicals, extremists, terrorists." He pauses. "But let me assure you that the nineteen hijackers were not Muslims, for Allah does not accept murder. They were misguided radicals who took pieces of the *Qur'an*'s teachings and twisted them to justify their own aggressive beliefs."

I wish Mom could hear this, but honestly, I think deep down she already knows. I look around. Most people are nodding. A lady next to me wipes away a tear.

Sheikh Muhammad continues. "The nineteen hijackers do not represent Islam, either. Our purpose today is to reach out—to help set the record straight."

I can see why Sam wants to be here—why he needs to know who he is.

I reach in my pocket and pull out Grandpa's medal. I have more questions for Mom, too. I want to know everything about the greatest man who ever lived, but I can wait till she's ready.

....

When Dad and I get home, Mom's on the couch reading.

I sit next to her. "I'm going for a run, okay? Maybe we can watch *Stuart Little* later?"

Mom closes her book. She's been taking her time answering any questions the last few days. It's like she wants to say one thing but stops herself and thinks first. It can't be easy for her. She told me her therapist said she shouldn't make her fears become my fears. I think he's a pretty smart guy.

She turns to me. "Please . . . please be careful."

I lean in and give her a kiss her on the cheek. "I will."

On the porch, I bend to tie my shoes. An American flag catches the wind and waves. It's not Grandpa's flag; his is sitting on my dresser. It's a flag Dad picked up this week from the hardware store. It makes me smile every time I step outside.

I pass the Wilkeys' on my run. There's a green Gatorade on the bottom step. I jog over and pick it up as Mr. Wilkey looks out the window. I raise the bottle in the air and mouth, "Thanks."

When I turn the corner, there's a black SUV in Sam's driveway. My heart almost stops. I stand on the sidewalk as Mr. Madina gets out of the back. In an instant, Mrs. Madina, Sam, and Aamber burst through the front door. They wrap their arms around him and he bundles them up.

If it were me, I'd never let go of him.

They head inside and I'm about to take off when Sam comes back outside holding something. He waves me over.

"Here, you should have this." He hands me his white captain armband.

"Does this mean you're not coming back to school?"

"I'm coming back, but you earned this, not me."

I flip it over a few times in my hand. I thought when I was finally made captain it would the best moment of my life, but so much has happened over the last few weeks that it's kind of dumb that I ever cared that much. "It's not a big deal."

"Look, you didn't bail on the team even when I did. Take it."

I shove it in my pocket. "Thanks."

Sam stops at the front door. "Come back after your run, okay? We're going to celebrate."

I head to the sidewalk and then run toward Mullins Park. The pavement is level under my sneakers. I whiz by the wooded path in Cypress Park on my way to Mullins' smooth track. There's nothing but me and wide-open space. Truthfully, though, it's kind of boring. I turn and run in the other direction. In front of me, branches stir. I'll have to be on the lookout for potholes and roots like land mines, but it's okay. I can take 'em. I dart into the woods, ready for anything.

ACKNOWLEDGMENTS

....

I could thank each person who has helped me along this crazy publication journey every day for the rest of my life and it would never be enough. But here's a start:

First, I'd like to thank two professors I was blessed to meet at the University of South Florida. Dr. Houston, you taught me the depth of books. And Dr. Cruz, you taught me to see the world in an entirely new way. I would never have written a book if our paths had not crossed.

Michelle Delisle, my critique partner and friend, I'm going to nickname you Hatter—you've worn so many hats with me. I truly thank God every day that He brought us together. You have been with me each step of the way, and there is no one I'd rather have by my side. I honestly think there were days that you thought longer and deeper about my novel than I did! You've unstuck me in the stickiest times and smacked me around when I needed it. Yep, Hatter!

Dorian Cirrone, I remember sitting in your COACH class at the library and thinking how ridiculously smart you were. Seriously, you know everything. I thank you for your friendship, for our almost weekly lunches, for your tough-as-nails advice that pushed me to be a better writer, and for your patience, as I slowly absorbed your expertise over time. Thank you for being the best mentor possible.

As a new writer, I was fortunate to have discovered Joyce Sweeney. Joyce, you were a constant cheerleader when I needed it most. Heck, you still are! Your enthusiasm for publishing is infectious. I'll always be grateful. Love, #41.

My fellow Wednesday-ers—Michelle Delisle, Mindy Weiss, David Case, Norma Davids, Danielle Joseph, Gina Albanese, Laen Ghiloni, and Nicole Cabrera—I loved sharing those mornings with you. Thank you for your inspiration. A special shout-out to fellow Wednesday pal, Christina Diaz Gonzalez, who provided my very fist blurb for the book and offered insight into immigration law.

To *all* my SCBWI conference pals, especially Linda Bernfeld and Gaby Triana, thank you for supporting me and celebrating with me. Where's the dance floor?

Jennifer Rees, it was fate that you attended the Orlando SCBWI conference all those years ago—though I'm still not sure how you think my dad is funny. You are crazy-talented. Thank you for focusing "fresh eyes" on my manuscript and for helping me figure out exactly what was missing. You are a puzzle master!

To my beta readers, most especially to my dear friends, Linda Benson and Cindy Gress. Thank you for encouraging me to add depth and richness to my story.

Mr. Khatib and Bushra Razvi, thank you for reading with an open mind, correcting my mistakes, and gently guiding me as I explored Islam.

Katy Betz, I knew the minute I met you at SCBWI a few years ago that we'd be friends. There's a deep goodness about you. And to be able to work on the cover of this book together—just wow. It's a dream come true. You are immensely talented. Stoked!

Mr. Richart—my former teacher and guidance counselor at Bishop Moore—thank you for seeing in me what no other teacher before had seen and for making me feel smart, despite my average grades. Though you are gone, your legacy lives on as Coach Rehart here on these pages. I hope, through this book, you will touch more children's lives.

There are many others who helped me complete this novel: Jim Greene, who allowed me to ask questions about the FBI; Jlal Khatib, who showed up at USF one day and instantly became one of my best friends; Representative Ari Porth, who gave me the scoop on being a Florida House Representative; and Brian Cognato and Peace Players International, who helped me understand how a game of basketball could bring kids together for a cause.

A *huge* shout-out to my Luv2Write girls! I would be in a million little pieces by now if it weren't for you all. Michelle Delisle, Kristina Miranda (Kris: my moral compass, grammar pro, SCBWI roomie, and decades-long friend), Jill Mackenzie, Meredith McCardle, and Nicole Cabrera—you are my glue! I will cherish you forever. And ever!

Liza Flessig, of the Liza Royce Agency LLC, super-agent-extraordinaire, my heart is forever grateful that you fell in love with Jake's story and made sure the world got a chance to hear it. I often reread your early emails where you gushed about "having" to represent this book. You've been my rock. Thank you! And thanks to the whole LRA gang, too!

To my amazing and brilliant editor at Sky Pony, Julie Matysik. You opened your arms wide to welcome Jake's story into your life. Thank you for loving him like I do and for convincing me that less is more. You were right!

To my entire extended family at Skyhorse/Sky Pony Press—being out on sub often feels like sitting under the

Sorting Hat in a *Harry Potter* novel. I landed in the perfect house for me. Thank you for taking a chance.

To my friends who have *truly* listened to me blab about my writing and yet still ask me about it each time we're together, thank you. It makes this job a lot less lonely!

To my brother and sister—thank you for believing in me. And Christy, thank you for letting me read to you every single night when we were kids. I often miss it.

To my parents and my grandfather—thank you for being the best examples of human beings I've ever met. By watching you, I've aspired to be the best version of myself. You are good through and through. Thank you for your unwavering love and support.

And finally, to Shawn, Kylie, Josh, and Griffin— thank you for your understanding during the long days (and often nights) I spent working on this book. Thank you for not letting me quit. And mostly, thank you for being my light, my hope, my world! I love you!!!

AUTHOR'S NOTE

············

In September of 2001, I, along with the rest of the world, watched in horror as the attacks unfolded on New York City and the Pentagon, and in the sky over a tiny Pennsylvania town. As heart-wrenching as it was to watch on TV—I was glued to my TV for days—I was also swept up with the sense of patriotism that swelled deep for months after. Everywhere I turned, red, white, and blue saluted people across town from T-shirts, to pins on our lapels, to flags boasting in the sky. Neighbors who usually came home, pulled into their garages, and closed the door never to be heard from, suddenly stopped in their front yards to talk. People came together in ways I'd never experienced before.

Within a day or two of the attacks, my alternating moods of anger, sadness, and pride suddenly had a new emotion to deal with. Fear. It was discovered that

Mohammad Atta, the hijacker of American Airlines Flight 11, lived just around the corner in my smallish town of Coral Springs, Florida—over 1,000 miles away from the closest attack. What if I'd seen him around? What if my family and I had eaten next to him at a restaurant? It stunned me to the core.

It didn't take long for more of the details involving that day to emerge. It seemed Atta and several of the other hijackers had made their way around South Florida unassumingly for months. But when it leaked that these men had taken flight lessons in Venice, Florida, and it was believed they'd had help from fellow Muslims living there, hundreds of what-ifs began to haunt me. Especially one pertaining to the parents of a friend I'd met in college.

My friend had come to the US to study and to get away from the strict Islamic rules of his upbringing, if only for a while. We grew so close that eventually my sister, my boyfriend, and I went to visit his devout Islamic family abroad, where his parents welcomed us into their home and treated us like old friends. A few years later, wanting to be closer to both of their boys who were then living in Florida, his parents decided to move to the states—Venice, Florida, to be exact.

In the days following September 11, I found myself doubting my friend. Doubting his family, who could have helped these terrorists somewhere along the way. Had they? I'd love to say my answer was quickly a clear no, but I'd be lying. It took a day or two for my head to clear and to be able to feel with certainty that they weren't involved. Not the loving, welcoming people who had become my friends. I hated myself for having ever wavered in my thoughts of them to begin with, but the emotion of that tragedy ran deep. The emotion controlled me.

Not long after, I talked to my friend and asked how he and his family were doing. He told me that the FBI had questioned his parents, and though they were cleared, life had become difficult for all of them. I listened to him talk, and though I didn't admit to him then that I had doubted them myself, he knows now. So do his parents, and I cannot thank his father enough for reading several drafts of this book and helping me get it right.

The feeling of regret stuck with me for a long time. Being a teacher, I looked at kids around me who rarely saw racial lines and I wondered, if this boy—my college friend—and I had been younger when September 11 happened, would I have ever doubted his family? Would I have had the prejudice that seemed to come with age? I began asking questions of anyone who wanted to discuss the subject. Soon I was taking notes, scouring the Internet, and reading books; amazed to learn that many non-practicing Muslim kids in the United States actually turned to mosques for answers following 9/11. The basis for my story developed in my head before I even realized I was writing it.

As a former history teacher, this was a story I knew needed to be told. It's the type of novel I myself would have used in a classroom to supplement the textbook and show kids, who didn't experience that day firsthand, the enormity of the event that happened on our own soil and took thousands of lives—six of them from my own small town, a thousand miles away. I want children to know that sentiments changed from minute to minute; teetering between patriotism, alarm, grief, and so much more. One of my favorite scenes in the book is the one where Jake and his dad attend a memorial service three days after 9/11. That event is real. It moved me the same way it moved Jake. I hope it moves you, too.

I'd like to note that the timing of the events in my book are real: the times of the planes hitting, the days and times of the president's speeches, and Tropical Storm Gabrielle that blew through Florida in the days following 9/11. Even the NFL canceling games that following weekend is true. However, the final mosque scene is entirely fictional. Though there were mosque attacks around the country, there were no mosque attacks in Coral Springs, nor is there a mosque in town. I took some creative licensing with that, in order to tell a story about where the road of prejudice can lead. The story of the mother is fictional, and yet her back story is based on a real American hostage incident that occurred in Sudan in 1973 and involved an Arab PLO terrorist group called Black September. The depth that the mother was able to add to this story, because of her past, is one I hope kids in classrooms all around the country will be able to learn from. We cannot let fear control us.

DISCUSSION QUESTIONS

....

For extension activities to use with this book, please visit the Teacher Resources tab at www.kerryomalleycerra.com.

1. A cover can tell a lot about a story. Study the cover of *Just a Drop of Water*. What stands out? How do you think the different elements on the cover tie into the story?

2. Some book titles are very commercial and tell you exactly what the book will be about. Others are more literary and make you think. Think about the title *Just a Drop of Water*. Does it give you any clue to what the book is about? What might be a good alternate title for this book?

3. From the very first chapter on, it's clear that Jake longs to be a hero. In what ways do you see him try to fulfill this desire? Do you think he's successful in the end?

4. Have you ever longed to be a hero? Describe what makes you heroic. What else have you longed to be?

5. In what ways does the author keep the tension rising as the book moves forward? Cite specific examples.

6. The author chose Jake to narrate the story. How do you think the book would have been different if it had been told from Sam's point of view? Is there another character you wish had told the story? Why?

7. The book is set in a small Florida town. Why do you think the author chose this setting? How important is the setting to the book?

8. Compare and contrast the siblings Sam and Aamber, especially noting their actions following September 11. Also compare and contrast Jake and Sam. Which character do you relate to most? Why?

9. The author states that the purpose of history is to learn from past mistakes and successes. Cite examples used in the text to make this point. Do you agree or disagree with the statement?

10. Based on the above question, examine the placement of Japanese Americans into internment camps during WWII. Compare and contrast this to the detainment of Sam's dad in *Just a Drop of Water*.

11. Describe the difference between tolerance and acceptance. Cite specific examples of intolerance, tolerance, and acceptance throughout the book. Where does Jake's mom stand on

this? How does her stance on this change throughout the book?

12. Explain how Jake responds to changes as the plot moves forward. Cite specific examples from the beginning, middle, and end to show his progression.

13. Jake and Sam endure much during the course of the book. Do you believe they'll stay friends? Why or why not?

14. What themes does this book explore? (Examples: fear, friendship, loyalty, peace) Choose one, and cite examples of this theme in the text. Why do you think the author chose to write about this? How does the theme progress throughout the book? How does this theme affect different characters? How does the theme affect the outcome of the book?

15. Cite different examples of cause and effect throughout the book.

16. The author arranges each chapter by calendar date rather than titles. Why do you think that is? Create your own chapter titles for the book and explain your reasoning for each.

17. Though Matt may seem like a small supporting character in the book, why do you think the author included him? What importance does he play?

18. Near the end of Chapter 8, Jake's mom is referring to Sam's family when she says, "No. But how well do we *really* know them?" What do you think propels her to say this? What do you think she means by it?

19. In fiction, it's important for a character to arc (change/ grow) by the end of a book. Make a list of the characters that help Jake arc. Pick your favorite and study in detail their role in Jake's growth.

ADDITIONAL RESOURCES

....

Mecca and Main Street: Muslim Life in America after 9/11 by Geneive Abdo

The 9/11 Report: A Graphic Adaptation by Sid Jacobson and Ernie Colón

Islam for Dummies by Malcom Clark

Muslims in America after The Catastrophic Tragedy of 9/11 by Edwin Ali

The American Muslim Teenager's Handbook by Dilara Hafiz, Yasmine Hafiz, and Imran Hafiz

With Their Eyes: September 11th—The View from a High School at Ground Zero Edited by Annie Thoms

Growing Up Muslim: Understanding the Beliefs and Practices of Islam by Sumbul Ali-Karamali

Sun-Sentinel, Broward County, Florida, issues September 12 through October 16

Miami Herald, issues September 12 through October 16